# AN IMAGE OF YOU

Millionaire Sir Charles Bainbridge, at the end of his patience with his daughter Georgette's behaviour, sends her to Kenya. Humiliatingly, she must work as an assistant to the ultimate male chauvinist Lukas on a location shoot. They met once before . . . in rather strained circumstances! In fact, she'd showered him with flour and he hadn't been pleased. And now she must be nice to him. This will take every ounce of acting ability Georgette possesses — and she is no actress.

LIZ FIELDING

# AN IMAGE OF YOU

*Complete and Unabridged*

**LINFORD**
*Leicester*

First published in Great Britain in 1992

First Linford Edition
published 2009

British Library CIP Data

Fielding, Liz.
   An image of you. - -
   (Linford romance library)
   1. English- -Kenya- -Fiction.
   2. Love stories.
   3. Large type books.
   I. Title II. Series
   823.9'14–dc22

ISBN 978–1–84782–903–0

Published by
F. A. Thorpe (Publishing)
Anstey, Leicestershire

Set by Words & Graphics Ltd.
Anstey, Leicestershire
Printed and bound in Great Britain by
T. J. International Ltd., Padstow, Cornwall

This book is printed on acid-free paper

# 1

'Lukas?' Georgette Bainbridge felt her mouth go dry at her father's suggestion. 'You want me to work for Lukas!' The day which had begun so badly suddenly became a disaster. 'You can't mean it!' But one look at his face confirmed that he did.

Sir Charles Bainbridge threw the morning paper across the desk at his youngest daughter, who stood facing him with clenched hands and a mutinous expression. 'I have had enough of this nonsense. It's time you stopped making a nuisance of yourself and a fool of me.' George didn't need to look at the newspaper. She had the most vivid recollection of the incident, and could still almost feel the imprint of the policeman's hand as he had manhandled her out of the road and into a van. And the reality of bruised

1

ribs from thugs who had caused the near-riot. Angrily her father jabbed at the paper. 'I've come to the end of my patience with you.'

'The end of your patience . . . ' she spluttered. 'Have you any idea . . . any idea . . . up here in your . . . ' she glared around at the opulent office ' . . . ivory tower . . . ' she brushed away his exclamation of rage ' . . . just what is going on down there?' She pointed dramatically at the window.

Her father's voice was icy. 'I have a great deal more idea than you do what is going on in this world. Tell me what your demonstrations do!' he challenged. 'Have you found one abused child a home? Have you, to your knowledge, saved one single whale?' he demanded. 'Have you provided one homeless family with somewhere to live?'

'Yes . . . '

'I exclude the army of people you seem to have installed in your own house!' George opened her mouth to protest, then closed it again. A row with her father wouldn't solve the far more immediate problem: to convince him that she couldn't possibly go and work for a man like Lukas. But she wasn't given the opportunity. 'Well? Have you no answer? It's unusual to find you lost for words, George.'

Shaken by his attack and tired from the night spent in a police cell, George subsided into the chair in front of his desk and let her eyes drop to the front-page headline: MILLIONAIRE'S DAUGHTER ARRESTED AT DEMONSTRATION.

She sighed. It had been a peaceful march until a bunch of louts had started jeering and pushing them about. Her first reaction had been to reach for her camera, but they had seized it and smashed it, and she had struck out in blind fury. It was so unfair.

'They broke my camera,' she said, with a surge of unaccustomed self-pity.

'I hope it was insured.' Her father's wry comment gave her pause. She hadn't expected him to be pleased with her. But it wasn't like him to be so angry. He was mostly amused by the scrapes she got into in pursuit of one cause or another.

She tried to rouse him to her side. 'That's not the point, Pa. Those bullies broke up a peaceful demonstration for no better reason than they thought it would be a bit of a lark . . .'

'Enough!' Her father was rarely roused to serious anger, but clearly this time he was not to be cajoled. She stopped. 'Thank you, Georgette.'

George cringed. If her father had stooped to calling her by that name she was in deep trouble. 'I'm sorry.'

Her father's smile caught her unawares. 'Of course you are. You are always sorry, George.' He stood up and walked across his opulent office to the wide windows looking out across the river. He recognised a certain truth in George's accusation that his office was an 'ivory tower', but he wasn't as cut off as she thought. He steeled himself to an unpleasant task, straightened his shoulders and turned to face her. 'I've lost count of the times you have come to me and said you were 'sorry'. You were sorry when you were expelled from boarding-school. Why was that, now?'

'Kittens. The gardener was going to drown the kittens,' she reminded him.

'Oh, yes, kittens.' The voice was heavy with irony. 'However could I have forgotten the kittens? You held a protest. Hung a banner across the school gates, set up a picket-line. Quite remarkable powers of organisation for a girl of thirteen.' He shook his head. 'What a waste. You could have been a captain of industry by now.'

George felt a bubble of indignation rising in her throat. 'There was no need to drown the poor little things. If they hadn't wanted her to have kittens she should have been spayed. Anyway, it would all have been a storm in a teacup if Heather James hadn't telephoned the *Sun*.'

'Your first headline. Tell me, do you keep a scrapbook?' George thought she caught a glimpse of a smile.

'No.' She shook her head.

'A pity. It would doubtless make entertaining reading.' He paused, frowning. 'If I were not your father.' She remained silent, hoping that he had finished. He hadn't. 'You were sorry when you were thrown out of art college. I was sorry about that too. They might have let you take your finals.'

'I finished the course,' she said defensively. 'Examinations are an archaic form of assessment.'

'Perhaps. You have great talent, George, and if you had had your 'archaic' piece of paper you might have developed it instead of spending your time with a bunch of . . .'

'They are my friends,' she defended them hotly.

'Hmm. Well, they are not the reason for this chat.' He paused. 'Are you aware that the cost of running that little house of yours in Paddington is almost as much as Odney Place?'

George winced. Her family home had

twenty rooms and a staff of five. 'I feed a lot of people,' she said, defensively.

'What on? Smoked salmon?' He suddenly thumped the desk, making her jump. 'You are twenty-two years old, George. Time enough to have learnt that you cannot personally take on the troubles of the world.' He backed off, seemingly embarrassed by his outburst. 'I'm sorry. But you can't. As for this latest plan of yours, wanting to break into your capital to build a refuge for the homeless . . . '

She stared at him. 'How do you know . . . ?' Then she brushed that aside as unimportant. 'I can do something, Pa. While you sit up here making money there are children begging on the streets!'

He sighed. 'There's a lot that's wrong with the world, George. But you'll never beat the system like that!' He waved his hand at the newspaper that lay on the desk between them. 'Have you no shame? Dear God, it was bad enough that you were arrested, but why on earth didn't you telephone? You didn't have to spend the night in gaol.'

'Would you have bailed out the others?' Her father didn't answer and she shrugged. 'I didn't think so.' George was tired and dirty. She was in desperate need of a bath to wash away the pervasive police-station smell of disinfectant that clung to her clothes.

She stood up and went over to him, taking his hand. 'Come on, Pa. It's not that bad.' There was a special smile that had never before failed her. But her father's eyes met hers blankly, refusing to respond.

'Not everyone has had your advantages, George. Some people have to go to work every day whether they want to or not. They don't have the luxury of a private income.' His eyes slid over her dishevelled appearance and he shook his head. 'Not that anyone would know. Why can't you be more like your sisters . . . ?'

George snorted. 'All tweeds and babies and dogs?' She caught her father's expression and held up her hands in mock defence. 'I know. I know. I don't appreciate you all, or how lucky I am . . .'

'Well, perhaps you can learn to. I have stopped your credit cards from today. And your bank account.'

There was a moment of stillness between them. George's thick dark brows drew together as she tried to take in what her father had said. 'How can you do that?' She shook her head. 'You *can't* do that . . . ' She pushed back long strands of hair that had escaped from her unhappy attempt at a French plait.

'It seems that I can. I have deemed that you are no longer . . . ' He paused, seeming to choose his words with care. 'No longer a fit and responsible person. I hope that it is a temporary aberration.'

'You can't do that!' She took in the implacable expression on her father's face, and her outrage turned to concern. 'I've bills to pay, responsibilities . . . '

'Bills will be paid under my signature.' He looked up. 'Your 'responsibilities' are living rent free. They will, for the moment, have to provide their own food.' Sir Charles opened the folder in front of him. 'You are more fortunate than most. I have, as I said, already arranged a job for you.' He looked up. 'I'm afraid it is only temporary as assistant to Lukas on a location shoot. But then beggars can't be choosers. Perhaps in Africa you will learn that there is worse to contend with than the welfare state.'

George sat down opposite her father and prepared at least to make a show of listening while she tried desperately to think of some way out of her predicament. One thing was certain — and her fingers strayed absently to her lips — there was no way that she could work with Lukas.

'Now, George.' Her father reclaimed her attention. She recognised the tone of voice. It was the one he reserved for particularly tiresome puppies. 'Your plane leaves tonight. A room has been

10

booked for you at the Norfolk Hotel in Nairobi . . . '

'Nairobi?' Her heart skipped a beat in sudden excitement.

'Mr Lukas will pick you up as soon as he can.'

His name brought her rudely back to earth. She shook her head. 'No. It's no good, Pa. Not Lukas. I can't work with him.'

'I don't remember offering you a choice, George.' Her father's eyes narrowed. 'I take it from all these protestations that you have already met the gentleman.'

'Gentleman!' That was the last thing she'd call him. And of course she'd met him. They had once had a memorable close encounter. One that she would heartily like to forget. There was nothing for it but to throw herself on her father's mercy. 'Please don't do this to me. I can't go! He's . . . '

'Yes?' Sir Charles waited.

She took a deep breath. 'I threw a bag of flour at him when he was judging an international beauty contest.'

Her father's laughter was genuine. 'I don't remember being asked to bail you out,' he prompted.

'He didn't press charges.' George refused to look her father in the eye. Lukas had dealt with her personally. Very personally.

Sir Charles Bainbridge looked at his daughter with interest. 'You'd better hope he doesn't remember the incident as clearly as you obviously do.'

She remembered. And she was sure he would. She felt hot tears of humiliation welling up behind her lids. Why couldn't he see that it was impossible for her? 'He's a dreadful man. Really. I won't go. I absolutely refuse.'

'Totally beyond the pale without a doubt. But a very fine photographer nevertheless. I am sure you can learn a great deal from him.' Her father came round the desk and leaned against it. 'This job will be a complete break from all this nonsense you've become involved in. Go willingly, George. And when you return, if you have done well . . . ' he raised a hand to prevent her interruption ' . . . I will be prepared to discuss your plans for a refuge.'

'Why?' she interrupted. 'Why now?'

Charles Bainbridge considered his favourite daughter. She was so like her mother, that high sense of justice. He sighed. 'You need a focus. You racket around endorsing any cause that takes your heart.' He smiled at her. 'It's a good heart, I don't deny it, but you're wasting yourself. Burning up your energy in too many directions at once.'

George saw a chink of light and dived in, sitting forward eagerly. 'But I could start right away. If you'll help I'll stay away from protest marches, I promise.' She smiled winningly.

'George!' She subsided back into the chair and shrugged. It had been worth a try. But her father had continued. 'I am asking you to do something for *me*. Something you're good at. Try and think of me as a deserving cause; that should help.' He too had a special smile to help him get his way. 'It's surely not much to ask in return for *that*.' He waved at the newspaper. 'Just do a good job for Lukas.' He tried to turn his order into a joke. 'Or he may refuse to work for me again. And that would make me very cross indeed.' He held out a folder containing her ticket. 'There are a few traveller's cheques with your ticket. Pocket money, that's all.'

She ignored the folder. 'And if I refuse to go?'

Her father shrugged, the smile gone. 'You had better hope that your friends are as generous to you as you have been to them.'

'I see. Cut off without a penny. Oh, well. I suppose there's always the DSS.'

Her father's eyes hardened. 'Don't you think they have enough calls on their resources already?'

George defied him for a long moment, then gave way before his determined look. 'You'll really help with the refuge?'

'You have my promise,' he assured her.

She took a deep breath. Her father's support would mean the difference between success and failure — a far more important consideration than her embarrassing encounter with Lukas. 'I'd better get going, then.' She picked up the folder, turned, hefted her battered leather sack over her shoulder, and walked briskly to the door where she paused and turned. 'And I am sorry about that. Truly.' She pointed to the newspaper.

'Keep Lukas happy and you're forgiven.' He smiled. 'Good luck.'

I've a feeling I'm going to need that, George thought as she closed the door. Keeping him 'happy' might not be that easy.

Her father's secretary handed her a longed-for cup of coffee. 'These are tablets to take against malaria, George. You should have been taking them for a couple of weeks, but follow the instructions on the bottle.'

'Thanks, Bishop. But it's not the mosquitoes I'm worried about.'

Miss Bishop laughed. 'You mustn't worry about Lukas, George. He is so charming. Not a bit the way they write about him in the papers.'

'Really?' George raised an eyebrow. 'I thought it was his 'charm' they concentrated on.'

Miss Bishop bridled. 'You know that you can't believe what you read in the papers.' She saw George's expression and had the grace to blush. 'Well, not everything. When Lukas telexed this morning for a replacement for Michael, I said to Sir Charles that it was just the thing . . . ' Her voice trailed off as she realised that she had given herself away.

'You suggested this? Oh, Bishop, I thought you were my friend.' She took the bottle of tablets. 'Why does he need a replacement?'

'He didn't go into details, it was just a short telex. But the poor young man who went out with him is in the hospital. Now I've bought you some sunblock creams and insect repellents. I didn't think you'd have much time. Is there anything else I can get you?'

George smiled. 'A new camera. Those beasts smashed mine yesterday.'

Her father's secretary looked doubtful. 'I'm not sure that I'm allowed . . . your father was most insistent . . . '

'It's covered by insurance. You can handle the claim for me, can't you? Dear Bishop? Please? I can't go to Africa without a camera.'

Miss Bishop relented. 'No, I suppose not. And if it's insured I'm not giving you cash, am I?' Having talked herself into helping, she handed George a notepad. 'Write down what you want. Henry can get it for you and he'll bring it when he picks you up to take you to the airport tonight.'

'Bless you. I shall need some film, too.' She startled the older woman with a hug. 'Here you are.' She quickly scribbled down the make and model.

'And some of these notebooks and pencils?'

Miss Bishop sighed. 'I'll send them with Henry. He's waiting to take you home now.'

'You're a brick!'

Once home — the little house in the back streets near Paddington Station she had bought a few months earlier — George let the bright mask slip. The place was a tip. The kitchen was full of her recent cell mates. They had eaten, and the debris littered every surface. George squeezed over to the fridge and as she expected there was nothing. Just an empty milk bottle. She wondered, not for the first time, if any of them had ever washed a plate in their lives, or gave a thought to where the food they ate came from. She sighed. If she had to squat in a condemned house, or live in a cardboard box, she probably wouldn't put washing-up very high on her list of activities either.

'Could someone get a pint of milk, please?' she asked as calmly as she could. She was ignored until she offered a note, then someone slid from a chair, pocketed the proffered cash and disappeared. She hoped he would come back with some milk. Change would be too much to expect.

She was so tired. They had spent the night singing protest songs, high on the adrenalin of arrest. But there was no time to sleep now. She would have to do that on the plane.

George unlocked her bedroom door. She wasn't quite as gullible as her father seemed to believe, she thought grimly. Her room was her refuge, inviolate, pristine, untouched by whatever disorder took over the rest of the house.

She stared for a moment in horror as she caught sight of herself in the bathroom mirror. Quickly she stripped off her clothes and dumped them in the laundry basket before stepping into the shower. It was fierce and reviving and afterwards she wrapped her hair in a towel, slipped into a wrap and went to examine her wardrobe, wondering just what would be appropriate for two weeks working in East Africa.

Her hand fell on the skirt she had worn to the beauty contest demonstration. A group of them had got in with tickets, pretending to be genuine spectators, and they wanted to look as if they belonged. They had decided on the role of models, hoping to attract attention. George had made the effort to look as stunning as possible, had secretly enjoyed it. She had worn a short black suede skirt and matching knee-high boots and she'd bought a cream silk shirt especially for the occasion. Then, because she was a perfectionist, even in the art of protesting, she had paid an unaccustomed visit to a hair salon, leaving after what seemed like hours, with her long hair a sleek gold curve over her shoulder. The final touch had been a professional make-up session. 'I want to look sexy,' she had told the girl tentatively, and she had been slightly shocked by the woman who had looked back from her mirror. Her violet eyes had looked sultry and twice their normal size, and her full mouth wider than she remembered.

Quite heady with the attention she had attracted when she arrived at the Albert Hall, she had played the vamp for all she was worth. And then Lukas had taken his seat among the judges and glanced around at the crowd. She had been in the front, her bag of flour concealed in the black suede fringed bag she had carried with her.

His eyes had fastened upon her with open appreciation as he took in every detail of her appearance in a slow and deliberate appraisal that made her blush to the roots of her beautifully *coiffured* hair. It was that look, the speculative lift of an eyebrow, that had made him her special target for the night. If he hadn't been so attractive she could have coped. But she found her eyes continually drawn to the magnificent black-clad shoulders, fascinated by the way his hair curled into his neck. Hoping and yet dreading that he would look at her again. And he had looked.

They had had to sit through the early rounds. As the girls had paraded in their national costumes and evening dresses Lukas had given her rather more attention than the contestants. She would have thought he was trying to pick her up if he had so much as smiled, but he hadn't. He had just stared. Well, she had shown him. That long moment when they were waiting for the result, when the television cameras had nothing special to look at, that was when they had struck with their bags of flour and soot.

But Lukas hadn't been a passive victim. He had grabbed a handful of her blouse and hung on despite her struggles until the buttons had given way. Instead of leaving it behind, and beating a retreat in her bra, she had tried to wrest it from him. Her efforts to cover herself had given him a second chance, and he had not wasted it. With one swift movement he had his arm around her waist, turned her over his knee and lifted that skirt. She shuddered at the recollection of his hand slapping her backside with considerable enthusiasm. Then, in the general pandemonium as the others had been arrested, Lukas had dodged the law and carried her backstage under his arm.

His black hair had been full of the flour she had dumped on him and as he shook his head a cloud of it rose around him and then descended over them both, coating his beautifully cut dinner-jacket. Her satisfaction had been short-lived.

'Are you going to scram, or do you want some more?' he demanded, as he finally handed her the treacherous blouse.

Scarlet, she struggled into it, clutching it around her. 'Why didn't you just leave me to be arrested with my friends?'

His eyes were like slate. 'Because, Miss Feminist, I prefer not to be the butt of the tabloids. I didn't duck out here to save you. If it was personal publicity you wanted, you should have thrown your flour at someone else. I'm going to clean up. That's the way out.' He pointed down the corridor. Trembling with rage and frustration, she raised her hand to slap him.

'Mr Lukas, sir, is that one of the trouble-makers?' A security guard had appeared behind her and she whirled round, but Lukas anticipated her intention of giving herself up and was too quick for her. His arm slipped around her waist and before she could protest he had pulled her close, holding her effortlessly.

'No. A friend, she's just leaving. Perhaps you would escort her safely to the rear exit? Just in case there are any more hooligans about.' She struggled angrily to free herself, but Lukas had no intention of letting her go so easily. Instead he bent swiftly over her and, realising his intent, she closed her eyes, desperately hoping that what she couldn't see wasn't happening. The first touch of his lips destroyed that illusion. This was reality with a vengeance. She had never been kissed to such effect before, or by anyone with the ability to turn her bones to putty. When at last Lukas had finished with her, she was too shaken to protest at his cavalier treatment. She merely sighed. He stared at her for a moment, his cool grey eyes shaded by unbelievably long lashes. 'There's hope for you yet,' he murmured finally, releasing her. 'Here, you'd better have this.' He slipped his jacket around her shoulders. Then louder, for the security guard, 'I'll see you later,' he drawled before disappearing in the direction of the dressing-rooms. 'Keep the bed warm, sweetheart.' And she had had to endure the sly smirk of the security man all the way to the exit.

George touched her lips in an involuntary gesture as she remembered that kiss. There was no reason to believe that among the hundreds of women who passed before his camera lens he would remember her, but it might be a good idea to disguise herself a little. Nothing obvious, just enough to avoid jogging his memory. One thing was certain — she wouldn't be taking that suede skirt with her.

Henry's eyebrows rose slightly as she opened the door to his ring and George had the grace to laugh. 'Don't look like that, Henry,' she begged.

'You took me back a bit, miss. I thought for a moment I'd come to the wrong house. I don't think I've ever seen you wearing a suit before.'

'And very uncomfortable it is too. If this is what is meant by turning over a new leaf, I shall be glad when it's spring.'

Henry took her bags and led the way down to the car. 'I'll keep an eye on the place while you're away, shall I?'

'Some of my friends are stopping there at the moment.' She saw the doubt in his face. 'They're not as bad as they look, really. But I've left some things for Miss Bishop in the hall; I'd be glad if you'd pick them up tomorrow. Did Bishop ask you about a camera?' she asked, changing the subject.

'It's in the boot. The receipts are in an envelope, for Customs.'

★ ★ ★

'*Jambo, memsahib.* Anything to declare?' George looked at the cheerful face, and gave herself a mental shake. She had slept the night away as the 747 had crossed Europe and half the length of Africa. She had missed a breathtaking sunrise over Sudan and left unopened the paperbacks she had bought at the airport. She had woken to steaming coffee and croissants, wishing heartily she had worn jeans and a sweatshirt instead of her now sadly crumpled suit.

The formalities of Customs took no time at all and soon George was being whisked towards Nairobi in a rackety Peugeot taxi decorated with red plush and gold fringes. She hardly had time for more than a glimpse of scrubby bush and distant hills before they were in the city, speeding along a dual carriageway lined with trees and parks, and punctuated by roundabouts dense with sculptured and exotic plant life.

On arrival at the Norfolk she was greeted by a vast Masai porter, six and a half feet if he was an inch.

'*Jambo, memsahib.*'

'*Jambo,*' George replied, quickly getting her tongue around the universal greeting and received a brilliant smile in return.

The receptionist too was welcoming. 'I've put you in one of the cottages, Miss Bainbridge, just through Reception, facing the garden. If you can fill in the registration form, please.'

'Of course. Am I in time for some breakfast?'

The receptionist checked her watch. 'Oh, yes. Another hour.'

'Great. I'm starving.' She signed the form and handed it to the girl.

'Your bags have been taken to your cottage. It's number three. Here's the key.'

George picked up the bag from the desk and turned to go. Then, with a sudden tremor, she stopped.

The tall figure seemed to fill the doorway. Cool grey eyes swept the small reception area, impatiently dismissing the airline staff and American tourists eager to be off on safari. Lukas headed for the desk, totally oblivious of the head-turning ripple that marked his progress across the room.

George watched his progress with apprehension. She remembered only too well that arrogant, hackle-raising assurance that was making the prickles stir on the nape of her neck.

Ridiculously she wished she'd had time to make herself look a bit more presentable. Her hair was everywhere, and she cursed her stupid suit to perdition. At least he would never connect the seductively dressed girl he had placed over his knee with this crumpled mess. But she grabbed the plain tinted spectacles from her bag and placed them on her nose as an extra precaution.

'I'm looking for George Bainbridge. He should have arrived this morning. Could you page him for me, please?' The receptionist stared, then giggled.

Lukas had been polite enough, but now he drew straight brows into a frown. Speaking slowly and carefully, as if she were slow-witted, or could not speak English, he tried again.

'I am Lukas. He is expecting me.' The girl looked at George and collapsed into speechless giggles, hiding the broad whiteness of her smile behind long brown fingers. He turned to follow her gaze and George could no longer postpone the moment. She firmly squashed the butterflies that were beating a tattoo in her abdomen and stepped forward.

'I think you must be looking for me, Mr Lukas. I am Georgette Bainbridge,' she said coolly. She extended her hand with a confidence she was far from feeling and trusted that he would not notice the slight tremor that seemed, quite suddenly, to have invaded her entire body.

For a long moment he stared at her. She shifted uncomfortably under his hard, unbelieving gaze. 'Everyone calls me George . . . ' Her voice trailed off uncertainly and she dropped her hand. He was obviously in no mood to take it.

His eyes travelled slowly from the toes of the plain black calf shoes, taking in the crumpled grey tailored suit and the white silk scarf that she had knotted so flippantly about her throat the night before, but which she was now aware looked merely rather sad. She had completed her transformation with a severe bun, from which wisps of hair were untidily escaping, and large tinted spectacles that were left over from the time she had suffered from an unsightly eye infection. The effect she had strived for was efficient and businesslike. But after sleeping in her clothes she looked anything but.

George was not unused to men weighing her up, assessing the possibilities, had seen Lukas do it himself. But he showed no such interest on this occasion. The curve of his mouth showed nothing but distaste and under his breath he murmured, just loud enough for her to hear, 'Oh, my dear God. What on earth have I done to deserve this?'

Stung, George was about to tell him. She opened her mouth, then remembered her father's words: 'Keep Mr Lukas happy and you're forgiven.' She wouldn't allow this wretched man to ruin her plans. She swallowed and instead forced a smile to her lips and said a little breathlessly,

'I'm afraid I've only just arrived. I was going to have breakfast. Will you join me, Mr Lukas?'

'Not Mr. Just Lukas.' His eyes, dark and intense under thick black brows, snapped with irritation. 'If you must eat, we'd better get on with it.'

The receptionist, having recovered from her giggles, was watching them with open fascination. Lukas glared at her and she rapidly found something of great interest on the desk in front of her.

George, infuriated by this unpleasant greeting, forced herself to stay calm. 'Well, I'm starving. Why don't you go in and order for us both to save time, while I wash my hands.'

He glanced at his watch. 'Please don't take too long, Georgette.'

George was quite firm. 'Not Georgette. George.' She picked up her bag and then couldn't resist a coy little wave. 'I won't be long.'

Her reward for this performance was to hear his barely contained explosive, 'God give me strength!'

Under the shower she veered between fury and amusement. Lukas clearly didn't like his women plain and untidy. Well, she didn't like him either. But for two weeks on location, photographing in Kenya, she would put up with a lot. And her father was right. He could teach her a great deal. So, while neither of them might like it, they were stuck with each other.

As she rifled through her bag, looking for something suitable to wear, she was almost sorry she had spent so much valuable time pressing her clothes. It would have been fun to change into something just as crumpled as her suit. She smiled wryly as she recalled that she had spent most of yesterday evening wishing she had taken more trouble with her wardrobe in recent months. Now her charity-shop bargains seemed to offer endless amusement. She slipped into a loose white T-shirt with a neck that had suffered somewhat in the wash. She had packed it to wear with her jeans, but they would be staying firmly at the bottom of her bag for the moment. Instead she pulled on a pair of well-worn green trousers that bagged at the knees, and she finished the look with an ancient pair of leather clogs that had once been expensive, but now were merely comfortable.

George surveyed herself in the mirror. Her deep gold hair was disguised in a neat if unbecoming bun. She teased a strand loose so that it would fall untidily with very little encouragement. Perfect. Her disguise seemed to take on a life of its own. Not quite grotesque. Just awful enough not to want to be seen with. Not, that was, if you were Mr Lukas.

# 2

Lukas was sitting facing the doorway of the dining room. He stared distractedly into space, his long fingers playing with a spoon and totally unaware of her presence. George paused in the opening and made a point of looking short-sightedly about her until she was sure she had attracted the attention of at least half of those present. As if suddenly aware that something demanded his attention, he looked up and saw her. It was a moot point whether he actually flinched, but George was not prepared to give him the benefit of the doubt. She waved enthusiastically and sailed towards him, firmly repressing the urge to try a theatrical 'trip'. There was a limit to what she might be expected to get away with.

'That's better.' She grinned widely

from behind her spectacles, keeping her amusement at the tight line of his mouth firmly under control. 'Have you ordered for me?'

'An English breakfast. You said you were hungry. You can help yourself to fruit or cereals from the buffet.' He carelessly waved at the laden tables in the centre of the dining room.

'Oh, how lovely!' she exclaimed as if she had only just noticed the lavish spread of tropical fruit. 'But I don't . . . That is . . . ' she stammered. 'It's all . . . rather strange to me,' she ended, peering anxiously at him from behind the spectacles, wondering how she had ever managed without such a wonderful prop before. 'Would you help me to choose?'

Lukas sat very still for a moment, and George could see the battle between his desire to strangle her and natural good manners pass briefly across his face. Good manners won, by a very short head.

'Of course.' He dropped his napkin

37

beside his plate and rose to his feet. She had forgotten how tall he was, well over six feet, and dwarfing her own feeble five foot six. He certainly attracted a great deal of attention as he led her around the buffet, showing her the different tropical fruits and attempting to explain the taste of papaw, mangoes, guavas and tree melons. She exclaimed loudly at these treats, feigned indecision and revelled in his embarrassment. 'Why don't you just try everything?' he said finally, allowing a hint of sarcasm to harden the edge of his voice.

'Oh, I couldn't!' George exclaimed, and helped herself to the slice of papaw she had always intended to have.

Once he had settled her back in her seat, and served her with hot coffee, Lukas cleared his throat. 'I'm afraid there seems to have been a slight misunderstanding, Miss Bainbridge . . . '

She interrupted. 'George. All my friends call me George, Mr Lukas, and

I am sure we're going to be very good friends.'

He declined to comment on that possibility and resumed where he had left off. 'I was expecting a man. When Miss Bishop telexed that I should expect George Bainbridge, I naturally assumed . . . '

George laughed loudly. 'You'd be amazed how many people make that mistake, but nobody ever calls me Georgette. Daddy always wanted a son, you see. I'm afraid all he got were daughters. Henry, Max and me.'

Lukas made a brave effort to recover from this revelation. 'The trouble is — er — George, it's going to cause some difficulty with the accommodation. Michael Prior was sharing a tent with me. And we don't have any spare room in with the girls.'

George choked on a piece of fruit and Lukas leapt up to beat on her back. Rather harder than necessary, she thought as she waved him away. 'I'm all right. Really.' Removing her glasses, she wiped her eyes, then sipped some coffee. She took a deep breath. 'Did you say *tent*?'

For the first time since they had met Lukas looked happy. As he resumed his seat he actually smiled. 'Yes. Two-man tents. Didn't Miss Bishop mention that?' He poured himself some more coffee. 'We're camped south of Nairobi, on the Athi River. Did you think we were shooting in Nairobi?'

George said nothing. She was speechless. She hadn't had much time to think about the shoot itself. She had thought her only problem was Lukas. But her father had known nothing of that incident. He did know, however, that she hated camping. That she loathed insects of any description and, worst of all, she was terrified of the dark. Pa was certainly getting his pound of flesh out of her.

Two weeks of Lukas, to ensure a better life for some youngsters who needed her help, had seemed a small price to pay. Too small. She should have known her father better than that. He was challenging her at long distance. How badly did she believe in her refuge? She drew in a deep, steadying breath. Badly enough.

'We may be able to get another tent from somewhere,' Lukas went on doubtfully, a speculative look in his eye, at her sudden pallor. 'Although we had the very devil of a job to get the ones we're using. But if you won't mind being on your own . . . ' Lukas helped himself to some toast, his appetite apparently restored. 'I suppose as long as you don't wander about at night you should be safe enough.' She stared at him as he bit into the toast, exposing a row of even white teeth, then shuddered. 'Do you normally wear glasses, George?'

'Glasses?' In her shock she had forgotten all about them. George ducked, quickly replacing her disguise. 'Oh, yes. Always. I can't do without them.'

Lukas shook his head. 'Just for the

moment I thought I had seen you somewhere before. The colour of your eyes is . . . unusual.'

'Perhaps we've passed in my father's office,' she said quickly, making a determined effort to pull herself back into her role. 'Although I'm sure I would have remembered,' she gushed.

'Your father's office?' She could almost hear the cogs working as he took in what she had said. 'Charles is your father?' He stared in disbelief. 'Miss Bishop said in her telex to expect a young relative of Sir Charles . . . but then I knew he only had daughters . . .'

'And you were expecting a man!' She forced herself to laugh out loud at this wonderful joke.

She saw a sudden spark of hope light his dark eyes. 'Well, Miss Bainbridge . . . sorry, George,' he corrected himself, making a belated attempt at friendliness. 'I realise that you can't possibly be expected to share a tent with me. It would be most improper. Your father . . .'

George found herself unexpectedly offered a getout. Lukas didn't want her. He would rather have no assistant at all than this badly dressed, unattractive creature. Her skill was of no importance to him, she reflected bitterly.

She could go home and say, quite truthfully, that when Lukas had found out that it was a girl they had sent him he had said no, thank you. But she had the strongest feeling that she wouldn't be believed. Who would believe such a ridiculous story? And Pa wouldn't keep his promise to help with the refuge. Oh, no, Mr Lukas, she thought as she sipped her coffee. You're not getting rid of me that easily. And she took comfort from the fact that her enforced presence on the shoot was as irritating for Lukas as it was for her.

Lukas had his hands on the table in front of him, his fingers laced together, his expression that of a man behaving with the utmost valour. George reached out and patted them kindly. Leaning forward, in a confidential tone she said,

'Do you know the very last thing Pa said to me yesterday? He said, 'George, keep Mr Lukas happy.' So don't you worry yourself a bit. It will be a relief to share a tent with you. I shall feel completely safe.' And that too was the truth, she thought grimly, firmly suppressing a shiver at the thought of being alone in a tent in the bush. Anything would be better than that. And she was sure that she would be perfectly safe from any unwanted attentions. There seemed little likelihood of Lukas making a pass at her. 'Oh, look. Here's breakfast.' She gazed at a plate piled high with more than she normally ate in a week for breakfast. 'Yummy,' she said, hoping the dismay she felt was not evident in her voice.

Lukas had obviously decided against a cooked breakfast. Instead he closed his eyes and leaned back in the chair, giving George a chance to study his face as she nibbled a slice of bacon. In repose he looked younger, less dangerous. And his eyelashes were scandalously long. It was a pity he wasted so much time on pointless work: calendars, pin-up girls, beauty competitions. A photographer with his talent and reputation could do a great deal of good with his camera.

'When you've finished we'll get off.' He hadn't opened his eyes and he made her jump. She wondered uneasily if he had been aware of her appraisal.

'So soon? I would have liked to see a little of Nairobi.'

'I'm not in the guided-tour business and this isn't a holiday, Miss . . . George. If you're going to be my assistant you had better accept that right now.' He had stopped being polite, lifting heavy lids slightly to see the effect his words were having on her. 'Preferably without having to be told twice.'

He had apparently decided that he was stuck with her. But he didn't like it. And she was ridiculously glad he didn't like it. But she kept her smile inside. She abandoned her effort to eat another sausage.

'I'll get my bags, then.' He stood up and she waited for him to offer to collect them for her. He didn't.

'I'll be waiting in the jeep. Don't be long.'

'No. At least I don't suppose it will take long to phone home, will it? I did promise Pa I would let him know I had arrived safely.' Some devil was driving her to annoy him, and she was unable to resist this last gibe.

Lukas placed his hands on the table and leaned across at her, his face very close to hers. She had time to notice that his eyes were grey, flecked curiously with blue, and they were surrounded by small white lines from being screwed up against the sun. It seemed unlikely that they were laughter-lines. A small muscle worked in his jaw.

'Miss Bainbridge,' he said heavily, 'I have wasted enough time today coming to Nairobi to fetch you. I'm going straight back. And if you are going to work for me, so are you. If your father wants to know that you arrived safely he will have to telephone the airline.'

George knew that she had gone too far. She wanted Lukas embarrassed, she wanted him unhappy. Angry she could do without.

'I'm . . . ' But he was in full flow and not about to be stopped.

'When I am working on location I work twenty-four hours a day. Seven days a week. And when I work, everybody works.' He let his words sink in. Then he continued with obvious relish, 'As my assistant you will be at my beck and call every moment of your waking life — and your sleeping one if I decide I need you in the night. So perhaps you had better decide where your priorities lie right now. I haven't the time to run back and forth to Nairobi so that you can telephone your father.' He stood up. 'I thought the man had more sense . . . ' he muttered.

She fumed inwardly. 'It's just as well we'll be sharing a tent, then,' she replied sharply. 'I can ask your permission when I need to use the lavatory.'

His eyes narrowed and, realising that she had let her disguise slip, she giggled and hiccuped. 'But I'd better not tell Pa. He might not understand.'

Like a drowning man, he clutched at the offered straw. 'You're right. He might not. Look, why don't you just stay in Nairobi for a few days? Have a look around. There's a lot to see. Just enjoy yourself. No one will blame you; it's well known that I've a short fuse. You could just say I was impossible to work for. There are plenty of people who would believe you.' He sounded genuinely sympathetic. He almost smiled. 'You can see how difficult it's going to be. That's the reason I prefer a male assistant. It will be very rough going, you know.'

Cruelly she snatched this straw from his grasp. 'Now, Mr Lukas . . .'

'Lukas, just Lukas!' he appealed.

'Oh, yes. Like 'just George'.' She giggled, again. 'Now Lukas, you remember what I said. Pa said I was to keep you happy. And keep you happy I will. However will you manage if you don't have someone to hold your light meter? I'll just go and get my bags, and then we can be off.'

'Hold my light meter . . . ?' For a moment she thought he was going to explode. Instead he straightened and with a shrug said, 'I'll meet you out front.'

And he was waiting impatiently behind the wheel when she returned. She threw her bags into the back and jumped up beside him. He stared in horror at the floppy hat she had added to her outfit with what, modesty thrown to the four winds, she believed to be a touch of genius. He opened his mouth as if to say something, then closed it again in a hard line.

'Well? What are we waiting for?' she asked with a happy smile. 'I thought you were in a hurry.'

He made no reply, started the jeep and executed a vicious U-turn before skidding away from the Norfolk Hotel.

They had travelled several miles

before he spoke. 'That is a terrible hat.'

George touched the offending head-gear. 'Oh. Do you think so? It's just to keep the sun off. This is hardly Ascot, is it?'

He gave her a sideways glance, taking in her motley attire, and grinned. 'Hardly. And I certainly wouldn't want you to get sunstroke. At least the other girls won't feel threatened.'

'Girls?' she repeated, refusing to get angry over his careless personal remark. After all, she told herself, she didn't care what he thought of her.

'They're highly strung creatures. They don't like competition from non-professionals.'

'I'm sorry. I don't understand. What girls?'

Lukas stared at her. 'The models. There are three of them. Kelly, Amber and Peach.' He sighed. 'For the calendar. Your father's calendar.'

'Calendar.' She breathed the word. It wasn't a question, because she knew now the full extent of her father's punishment. And half an hour ago she could have escaped. But not now. Now she was headed towards some unknown camp with Lukas. She had a few traveller's cheques, but no return air ticket, no way of getting home without throwing herself upon her father's mercy. And that she was not about to do. She was trapped and she would have to make the most of it.

'Yes, calendar. Didn't your father tell you?'

She shook her head. 'He was having a little joke with me. He has quite a sense of humour.'

Lukas glanced at her and almost smiled. 'Yes, I'd agree with that. So, tell me what you know about photography. What you've done.' He added, a little grimly, 'If anything.'

She didn't answer immediately, couldn't trust herself to, and she dug her nails into the palms of her hand to stop herself saying exactly what she thought. Lukas, it seemed, was in no hurry; his expression was unreadable as he waited for her to collect her thoughts. She sat desperately trying to think of something clever to say as Nairobi dipped below the skyline behind them and they began to drive eastwards across the empty plain.

For a while she had been enjoying the little game she was playing, but suddenly it wasn't a game. She stared out at the wide horizons, looking for inspiration. The hills over to the right were hazy blue, and the plain rolled away from them. It was vast, beautiful.

George gave herself a mental shake. What on earth was she complaining about? Perhaps being a colourless doormat under the feet of Lukas for two weeks was more than flesh and blood would be able to sustain. But she would certainly try. And she might as well get some amusement from it.

'I've taken lots of family photos,' she said, hesitantly, making sure to keep her face quite serious. 'The dogs. My sister's babies.' She stole a glance at Lukas. His face was set and hard as he took in her answer. 'They are very good. Everyone says so.'

'Dogs and babies.' His voice was expressionless. 'I see. Anything else?'

She pretended to think. 'I took a photograph of the Princess Royal once.'

'Oh?' he said, rousing a little more interest.

'Yes. She came to open a new wing at school. Of course she was just Princess Anne then . . . I sent her a copy that I printed myself. She wrote and thanked me.' She counted to three silently. 'At least her lady-in-waiting did. I kept the letter in my scrapbook. It's very hot, isn't it?' She fanned herself with her hand.

They were descending now and it was a lot warmer. The air had changed from the sharper clarity of the high plateau and there was a warm mustiness about it.

'It would have been cooler travelling if you hadn't wanted to eat,' he replied with some justification. 'And it will get a lot warmer than this. Nairobi is six thousand feet above sea level, and we're dropping down three thousand feet.'

'How long will it take to get to the camp?' she asked, looking around her and spotting with surprise and pleasure a herd of gazelle grazing near the road.

'That depends on the traffic.'

'On what?' She gasped, her attention re-directed towards Lukas. 'What traffic?' The road stretched away straight and clear before them. They were passed only by an occasionally over-loaded taxi being driven at a ridiculous speed, and saw the occasional truck driving towards the capital.

'Not cars or lorries. I was thinking of the odd elephant who didn't want to get out of the middle of the road.'

'You're joking!'

Satisfaction that he had managed to dent her confidence was written in every line of his darkly tanned face. 'I once had to back five miles down the side of an escarpment, just because an elephant decided it wanted to walk in that direction,' he said softly. 'But not more than a couple of hours, I suppose.'

'Where was that?'

Lukas glanced across at her. 'The elephant?' She nodded. 'Down on the Zambezi.'

Not here. Relief swept over her. 'And were you taking photographs for a calendar there as well?'

A sudden grin transformed his face. 'I could have done. There were a lot of very pretty girls.' Then the smile faded. 'I was there taking some publicity photographs for Save the Children. They were trying to raise money for polio vaccine.'

'Oh.' George was silenced.

Lukas frowned. 'That surprises you?'

'No. I hoped that was what you were doing here.'

'I see. Well, I'm sorry. You'll have to take it up with your father . . . it's his calendar.' He glanced at her with a slightly puzzled look. 'It beats dogs and babies any day of the week.'

Knowing the lengths she had had to

go to produce the portraits of her nieces and nephews, George didn't doubt it, but that was not what he meant.

'Babies and dogs are harmless,' she countered sharply, and regretted it before the words were half out of her mouth.

'Some babies, and some dogs,' he said coldly, and they drove on in silence for a while until they reached a bridge. Lukas pulled over, climbed down and held out a hand to assist her.

'Why have we stopped?'

'I'm indulging you in a little sight-seeing,' he said, although there was something about the glint in his eyes that belied that statement. 'You did want to do some sightseeing, didn't you, George?' Hesitantly she placed her hand in his and allowed him to help her down. For a moment they stood in the baking sun, and George was acutely aware of Lukas's scrutiny, and his warm fingers holding on to her hand. Glad of the protection of her glasses, she broke away from his piercing look and glanced about her.

'Well? What are we supposed to be looking at?'

'That,' he replied, pointing to another bridge a little way up the river. 'It's the Tsavo railway bridge.' She nodded uncertainly, wondering what could be so special about a very ordinary steel railway bridge.

'It's lovely. Thank you for showing it to me.' She turned to climb back up into the jeep. He had kept hold of her hand, tightening his grip.

'Surely you've heard of the man-eaters of Tsavo?' he asked. 'Or didn't you do your homework before you came on this trip?'

'I wasn't told until yesterday that I had to come.'

'Told?' He shrugged and didn't wait for a reply. 'They were a pair of lions who killed and ate more than a hundred men working on a railway bridge.'

'Good gracious,' George said with polite interest.

'That's the bridge. I thought you'd be interested.'

'Oh, I am. I love those old stories. They exaggerate so wonderfully.'

He laughed. 'You think I'm exaggerating, do you? It held up the railway for over a year. There's an excellent book about it. A personal account written by the chief engineer. I'll lend it to you if you think you'll have the time to read it.'

She gave him a long measured look but the hard profile gave nothing away. 'Thank you.' Lukas allowed her to pull herself free and she climbed back into the jeep, still not quite sure what Lukas was driving at.

'They dragged one engineer right out of a railway carriage,' he said as he pulled himself into the seat alongside her. 'But most of the victims were Indian workers asleep in their tents.' He laid the slightest emphasis on the word tent. He said no more, but gently let out the clutch and drove on. 'Of course lions aren't necessarily the most dangerous animals in the national park. There are some very nasty *dudus*.'

'*Dudus?*'

'Insects, bugs, creepy crawlies. It's the Swahili word.'

Feeling cold and clammy, George wiped away the sweat that was gathering under the unaccustomed spectacles. Aware that Lukas was regarding her discomfort with some pleasure, she made an effort to pull herself together. 'Oh, just look at that road sign. 'Beware. Elephants.' Just like ponies in the New Forest.'

Lukas turned to her impatiently, but before he could make some caustic remark his focus shifted and he slowed the jeep.

'What is it? Why are we stopping?'

'Quiet. There are elephants ahead. They're probably just going to cross.' He gently eased the jeep into reverse in case the herd decided to investigate them.

'Don't be silly . . . ' George started, sure she was being made a fool of. But suddenly she could see them. Just on the edge of the road, merging into the green-grey scrubby trees, she caught the dangerous lifted curve of ivory and the slow movement of great ears. 'Oh, but that's incredible.' Then, aware of his scrutiny, said inanely, 'You mean they cross just where there's a sign? How clever.' Then she abandoned her tiresome *alter ego* and, longing for her camera, turned to reach her bag in the back, cursing herself for not loading some film before she left.

'Be still!' Lukas hissed between his teeth, catching her arm and forcefully propelling her back into her seat.

'But I just . . . oh, look there's a little one . . . ' Then one of the largest animals turned to face them. She stepped forward, waving her great ears.

'And quiet! This isn't a zoo!' George subsided immediately, not needing to be told twice that the animal was threatening them. She had to content herself with watching the herd silently cross the road, and just for the moment she was glad she wasn't on her own despite the humiliating way that Lukas gripped her arm. Above the smell of hot oil and dust she could detect the faint scent of his cologne and she tore her eyes from the herd to regard her adversary.

The contrast with their previous meeting was startling. On that occasion he had been all smooth and manicured charm in an expensive dinner-jacket and snowy dress-shirt. His dark, almost black hair, despite its dousing with flour, had been fresh from a stylist who knew his job. Now, too long for elegance and damp with the heat, it had resumed a wayward curl. Sweat trickled down the side of his face and damp patches stained the sleeveless jacket he wore open over a short-sleeved shirt.

George wondered where he had come from. The name — Lukas — the faint trace of an accent, suggested eastern Europe.

He turned and caught her staring.

For a moment he held her gaze, then abruptly he let go of her. 'They're almost across.'

She rubbed her arm where his fingers had bit into the flesh and blushed, feeling foolish. She jumped as one of the beasts turned and bellowed at them, raising its trunk, before turning and disappearing with the rest.

When they had gone Lukas slowly moved forwards. George peered somewhat nervously into the bush on the side of the road as they passed, but there was nothing to threaten them. The elephant had gone. She sat back against the rock-hard seat. 'They're so big,' she breathed. 'Does that happen often?'

'I suppose so. But you were lucky to see it. And it's an ancient elephant crossing. The sign was put there to warn humans, not instruct elephants. You'd better have your camera ready in future, just in case your luck holds.'

'I'll keep my fingers crossed,' she promised. And my toes. And my eyes

. . . She giggled and was aware of an irritated exclamation from Lukas, but she didn't care.

'It's quite difficult to take photographs with your fingers crossed. But I'm sure you know that.'

The sun rose higher, and the heat increased in direct proportion.

For the first time, George wondered what exactly lay ahead of her. She had been too tired the day before to worry about it, and her confrontation with Lukas had given her no time for thought. But, as well as Lukas, out here were snakes and spiders and lizards and, apparently, lions.

The thought caused a crawling sensation at the base of her spine. She desperately wanted to turn and check that there was nothing in the jeep with them, waiting its moment to grab her by the neck and drag her away. She broke into a sweat as she considered that this was full daylight. Whatever would it be like at night?

She kept her face determinedly

forward, refusing to give in to nameless fears.

'Hold on!' The warning came barely in time. She was half jolted from her seat as Lukas swung the jeep off the road into the bush and over the railway line. There was a group of huts, a tiny store, a flurry of chickens and a glimpse of almost naked children staring with solemn black eyes as they swept past.

'Say goodbye to civilisation,' Lukas said with a grin, as they bounced along the road. Road! George caught her breath as the jeep slammed into a rut and bounced out again, lifting her clear of her seat. Lukas seemed not to notice, but then he had the steering-wheel to hold on to. She clung to her seat as they bounced along, leaving clouds of red dust in their wake.

A deer flew across the road in panic, practically jumping the jeep's bonnet, and George let out a small shriek.

'It's only an impala,' Lukas mocked. 'You get used to them. You'll see all sorts of creatures if you keep your eyes open. Foxes, jackals . . . '

'Lions?' she asked crossly.

They hit another rut and he didn't answer. George allowed herself a little inner feeling of satisfaction. He must be mad, thinking he could scare her with man-eating lion stories. She wasn't scared of lions. *Dudus* were something else.

'We're nearly there.' He slowed the jeep and George could see, in the distance, a greener patch of vegetation. 'The camp's on the other side of the river.'

The 'river' lay in a deep gorge carved out by rainy season floods, but now was nothing more than a few small trickles of water meandering between broad sand banks and only occasionally widening into pools. Lukas approached the bank with care. 'It's a good job for us the rains weren't bad. Otherwise we would have to cross by dinghy.'

'I've no objection to getting my feet wet in a good cause,' George said flippantly and immediately wished she hadn't.

'That's a statement you may live to regret, George.' Lukas smiled at some private thought as they tilted down the seemingly vertical drop. George hung desperately on to the jeep's dash until they reached the bottom, where they splashed through the small streams. Then he attacked the far bank. For a moment George thought they were not going to make it. She held her breath as the jeep seemed to hang suspended without the power to get to the top. But suddenly they were there. Wherever 'there' was.

'Welcome to Kathekakai,' Lukas said expansively, indicating the few tents with a wave of his hand.

'Kathekakai.' She said the word slowly, rolling it around her mouth. It had an almost magical sound, conjuring up witch doctors and ritual dances. 'What does it mean?'

'Place of Dread. Or Place of Killing — take your pick,' Lukas said matter-of-factly.

George stared at him, trying to decide

if she was being wound up again. But he had climbed down from the driving seat and was striding towards a large open-sided mess tent where several people were sitting. Feeling suddenly very alone, she scrambled down and ran after him, trying not to think what might be in the dry grass.

There were about half a dozen people sitting around a table, playing cards. They called out a greeting to Lukas, but their attention was caught by George. Lukas turned and caught her arm to pull her forward.

'Ladies and gentlemen, I present George Bainbridge,' he said with a flourish.

There was a sudden silence and a man, thick-set and middle-aged, who had his back to her, turned, stared for a moment then suddenly grinned.

'Good God. It's a girl.'

'I'm relieved you know the difference, Walter,' Lukas said drily.

'Oh, I've always known the difference, dear boy.' He came towards George and held out a hand in welcome. 'Take no notice of Lukas. I believe he practises being horrible in front of a mirror.'

A striking brunette, who had looked up at George's arrival, looked away again. 'I think I'm up. Four kings and a run of hearts.' She laid some cards out in front of her.

George felt a pulse beating in her neck. There had been a casual insolence, a dismissal of something without interest, about the girl's attitude. She made a very special effort to focus her mind on why she was here, in this Place of Dread, fixing her thoughts on the youngsters living in cardboard boxes and how much they would love to feel this sun, how lucky they would think her. She allowed her face to relax into a smile and stepped into the shade of the tent. 'It seems there has been a bit of a mix-up. I'm Georgette Bainbridge. Everybody calls me George.'

'Are you related to Sir Charles?'

'She's his daughter, Walter.' And George sensed rather than saw the look that passed between them. 'Is there anything to drink? What would you like, George?'

'Mineral water?' she asked, and was promptly handed a glass of ice-cold water.

'Thank you.' She drank it down in thirsty gulps and almost felt the steam rising. 'I'll get my things from the jeep, if someone will show me where to put them.'

'Come on, I'll give you a hand,' Walter said, then, as an afterthought, 'Where's she sleeping?'

'There's only one spare bed,' Lukas reminded him without expression.

Walter stared, then shrugged. 'I hope you know what you're doing, Lukas.'

'She'll be safe enough. Lukas has exquisite taste in women,' the brunette put in, invoking a loud shushing from another girl, and a fit of giggles from a youth.

'Come on, George.' Lukas took her arm and marched her across the camp. Stonily he took her bags from the back of the jeep.

'I can manage them,' George protested as he carried them across to the nearest tent. He held them in one hand as he unzipped the tent fly and then, ducking inside, he dumped them on one of the two camp beds. After a moment's hesitation George followed. She gasped as she took in a lungful of the stifling air inside.

'Dear God, however do you sleep in this?' she demanded.

'It's not so bad at night, but we keep the tents closed to keep the bugs out.'

She hoped he hadn't heard the involuntary choking sound from her throat as he unzipped the rear and held open the flap for her. But he glanced back. 'Are you all right?' She nodded. Apparently without conviction. 'Just remember to zip up after you and nothing can get in.'

'I won't forget,' she said, unable to suppress a shudder.

'There's a little wash area out here. The mess boy brings some water in the morning and evening.' He looked in the metal jug. 'There is some here if you want to freshen up. The shower takes a lot of water-carrying for the boys, so there's a rota and a time limit. And I'm afraid the models get priority. We'll have a programme meeting as soon as you're ready.' He turned to go, then paused, his back to her. 'I'll try and rig up some sort of screen in here if you like.'

'Thank you. If you'll just give me a minute to wash my face . . . '

He let the tent flap fall and disappeared. With relief George pulled off the hat and subsided on to the bed, her knees almost touching the one that Lukas slept in. The space was very hot and very small. The two of them standing up had completely filled the tent, and George wondered how long it would be before Lukas remembered where he had seen her before. She couldn't sleep in her glasses, or keep her hair in a bun day and night. The sooner he rigged up a screen, she thought, the better.

# 3

George stripped and washed, grateful to get rid of the dust that seemed to penetrate every crease. Her skin felt tight from the long hot ride in the jeep and as she searched in her bag for a moisturiser her hand fell on the sun-block that Miss Bishop had bought. She unscrewed the lid and grinned. It was the pale green stuff. Oh, lovely Bishop, she thought, hugging her mentally. She lavished on her moisturiser and then carefully stroked the green zinc oxide down her nose.

She glanced in the mirror. 'If you were vain, Georgette Bainbridge, this would be good for your soul,' she sternly told her reflection.

She stuck her hat back in place. Lukas was right, it was a truly dreadful hat. She couldn't even remember where it came from. She might frequent the charity shops, but that didn't mean she had no taste. She replaced the glasses, squared her shoulders and pinned a smile firmly to her mouth, and with her pale green nose as high as it would go she emerged into the brilliance of an African noon.

At her appearance the buzz of conversation died away. Clearly they had all been discussing her arrival. Lukas made a move towards her and then checked mid-stride, clearly struck dumb by the green nose. Walter was the first to recover.

'Well, here is the surprising George,' he smiled, showing even capped teeth, white against a suntan, which in turn set off his silver hair to perfection.

'Surprising?' She forced a giggle. 'Oh, because I'm a girl!'

Walter raised an eyebrow very slightly, but otherwise was unaffected. 'Let me introduce you to everyone. I'm Walter Burnett, artistic director of this fiasco. Suzy is our wardrobe lady.' George shook hands with a bird-like woman in her late forties, who smiled absently.

'Welcome.'

Walter carried on. 'Mark is our make-up artist. And Kelly, Peach and Amber are the reason we are all here. Come and sit down. We were looking at the sketches.'

George sank into a wooden folding chair beside Walter and glanced through the sketches of the planned photographs. The pictures certainly came under the heading 'glamour', but artistic glamour, she noted with relief.

'Which one will we be shooting first?' she asked.

'We've found the perfect site for this one.' Walter pulled a sheet from the bottom of the heap.

George looked at a rough sketch of Kelly stretched out upon a rock. 'Suzy is in charge of wardrobe?' she asked. 'Whatever does she do?'

Walter laughed. 'Well, there's the beautifully draped native cloth, and some beads . . . It is this photograph with the beads, isn't it, Lukas?'

George jumped as Lukas put his hand on her shoulder and leaned across her, turning automatically to face him. He looked down into her eyes and grinned. 'Yes. This is the one with beads.' He pulled out the chair next to her and sat down, leaving his arm draped across her shoulder.

'They're not beads,' Suzy said, looking up from some sewing. 'They're nuts, cogs, that sort of thing. Spare bits of cars and motorbikes. That's what the calendar is advertising.'

'Spare parts?'

'Surely you knew that?' Walter asked curiously. 'Your father is our client.'

George felt stupid. 'I don't have very much to do with the business,' she muttered.

'I don't think George altogether approves of us,' Lukas said with amusement. 'She thinks we should be taking earnest photographs for the *National Geographic*.'

'What's so funny about that?' she demanded.

'Nothing. Do you usually paint your nose green?'

'If I feel the circumstances demand it.'

His eyes glinted. 'What circumstances have driven you to it this time, I wonder?' She opened her mouth to reply, but he stopped her. 'Not now. I don't feel that strong.' He turned to Walter. 'You've found a site for this shot?' And the business of sorting out a new programme after the hold-up kept them busy until lunch.

George, once everyone had helped themselves from the cold buffet, stood uncertainly, balancing her lunch in one hand and a glass of mineral water in the other. The others had settled themselves in little groups and she felt excluded. She caught a sudden movement out of the corner of her eye and something hurtled passed her face, snatching a tomato from her plate. She let out a yell.

'Perhaps you'd better sit down. The monkeys think you're offering them a free dinner.' He pulled out a couple of chairs and sat down beside her.

'Sorry, it startled me.'

'And that was just a monkey,' he teased. 'What's the matter with the food?' he asked, after a moment, realising she was not eating.

'I'm not very hungry,' she said, letting the fork fall on her plate. 'I had rather a large breakfast.'

'Not that much. You left most of it.' He carried on eating. 'Just make sure you drink plenty of liquid.'

'I will.' She sipped at her glass of mineral water, half wishing Lukas would join the others and leave her alone.

'It's difficult, isn't it, George?' She started at his words; it was almost as if he could read her mind. 'Coming into a team that is already working together.'

'Oh, yes. I suppose it is.'

'We've been working on this project for quite a while, off and on. Relation-ships are already formed, friendships made.' He indicated the groups under the trees chatting easily together. 'They're a good bunch, but they don't know you. I don't know you.'

George knew he was getting at something, but couldn't quite put her finger on what. 'I realise that.'

Lukas nodded. 'Good. In that case you'll understand my concern that your arrival doesn't cause any problems. It's tough enough doing one of these jobs, without unnecessary upsets.'

She was now completely at a loss. 'I just came to do a job. I have no intention of upsetting anyone . . .'

'A job you know precious little about.' He ignored her protest. 'I don't know why it is that you bother me so much, George. At first glance you look too stupid to be trouble. Perhaps that's it. You seem to have taken such pains over it. The nose is perhaps a bit over the top, though, don't you think?' He ignored her sharp intake of breath. 'I was expecting a professional, you see, but if your father has sent you I have no choice but to respect his wishes. After all, he's the piper.' He stood up.

George clamped down hard on the impulse to tell him exactly what she thought of him. Instead she affected a puzzled expression. 'What makes you think I'm not a professional?' she asked quietly.

Lukas shrugged. 'Because you don't have to work. You can pick and choose what you do. That's the difference, wouldn't you say, between an enthusiastic amateur and a professional?'

'Perhaps,' she conceded.

'A working lunch?' Walter intervened, helping himself to another drink. 'Don't let Lukas work you too hard, George. He can be a slave-driver when he's got the bit between his teeth.'

'Hard work never hurt anyone,' Lukas said, with an emphasis that George felt was directed straight at her.

'So they say. But it doesn't do to take chances, dear boy,' Walter said smoothly. 'But we'd better get going if you're hell-bent on shooting this afternoon.'

'Of course we're shooting this afternoon. There are better things to do with life than sit around under a fever tree and waste time. Come on, George, let's see what's under that hat of yours.' He walked swiftly away, leaving Walter with eyebrows raised in genuine surprise.

'Well, George. What a very invigorating effect you're having on the boss. But don't you think you'd better follow him? He'll be looking for someone to fling orders at.'

George sighed. 'So long as that's all he flings,' she said, and set off in his wake. She found him in the store tent checking his camera and lenses.

'What took you so long?' He indicated a small refrigerator. 'Load some film. A couple of Polaroids. And some transparencies. It'll help keep the film cool if we do it in here.'

George, on safer ground with the nitty-gritty of photographic hardware, deftly did as instructed and placed the backs carefully in the cold bag, aware all the time that Lukas was covertly watching her. 'What next?' she asked.

He picked up a light meter and slipped the cord over her head. 'Look after this. Don't lose it,' he warned. 'If a crocodile swallows it, I expect you to go in after it.' He was standing very close, almost touching her, and she felt her breath tightening, a flush darkening her cheeks.

'Is that what happened to your last assistant?' she asked flippantly.

His fingers were still on the cord and they tightened. 'It's an odd thing, George. I could have sworn you wouldn't have known a lens from your elbow when I saw that brand-new camera you brought with you. Perhaps I was wrong.'

George almost relaxed. So that was what all this aggravation had been about. 'I had a bit of an accident with my own camera a couple of days ago. I didn't want to come to Africa without one.'

His eyes narrowed, and he demanded

anxiously, 'An accident? What happened to it?'

It was thrown to the pavement and two large men took it in turn to jump on it. No, she definitely wasn't going to tell him that. 'I dropped it,' she hedged. It wasn't exactly a lie. That brute had barged into her and she had, well, dropped it.

'Dropped it?'

'It was insured,' she said reassuringly, as she realised that he was staring at her horror-struck.

'Just make sure you don't have 'a bit of an accident' with mine,' he warned. 'No amount of insurance will save you from the consequences.'

'I'll be very careful,' she promised, as he released the cord and let her go. And she would be. There was an animal force about him that made him as dangerous as any crocodile. She had experienced his annoyance once before, but she had the feeling that the loss of his camera would upset him a great deal more than a bag of flour.

They loaded the jeep in silence while the rest of the team climbed up front. 'Michael used to sit behind with the equipment,' he said half apologetically as George realised that with Lukas driving there would be no room for her on the seats.

She shrugged. 'Whatever Michael can do,' she said, and climbed up among a jumble of cold bags and other assorted clutter.

Kelly turned round in the back seat and smiled. 'Are you all right back there? We could squeeze up.'

'She'll be fine,' Lukas assured them, as he shut the door on her. 'Won't you?' She glared at his retreating back.

George had thought it was bumpy riding in the front of the jeep, but it was nothing to sitting on the floor in the back as he bounced over the rough track. By the time she climbed down, stiff and aching, every bone in her body felt bruised from the jolting ride.

She stood and stretched her limbs for a moment, trying to get the circulation flowing in a normal direction. Lukas appeared beside her and shouldered the drinks bag and the tripod.

'This is as far as we can get with the jeep. We walk the rest.' With that he turned and scrambled down the river bank, helping the models, his voice floating back to her. 'Take your time, girls, I don't want any bruises.'

George picked up the cold bag with the films and the camera case and looked down the steep bank. There was no way she could manage to carry everything down at once and arrive in one piece. Aware that Lukas was watching her, waiting for her to ask for help, she put the film box down and carried the camera box carefully to the river bed. Ignoring him completely, she repeated the journey, by which time she was hot and breathless and painfully aware of damp patches on the back of her floppy T-shirt and dust-covered trousers.

But there was no respite. 'About time,' Lukas drawled, and set off at a pace that his long legs made deceptively fast. Her arms felt as if they were being dragged from their sockets and her legs were continually bumped by the load she carried.

On either side of the river bank were tall trees, with a sickly green bark. 'Did you call those fever trees?' she asked finally, to break the uncomfortable silence.

'It's just a local nickname,' he replied. 'Early travellers in these parts camped by the water where the trees grow, and then went down with malaria. They didn't know about mosquitoes. They thought the trees were the cause.'

'Who could blame them?' George shuddered.

Mark had dropped back beside them. 'I'll carry that for you,' he offered and took the cold bag containing the film.

She smiled. 'Thanks.'

Lukas glared at him. 'The going a bit tough for you already, George?' he asked, and picked up the pace until she was half running.

'Just a trifle warm,' she panted.

The party had in fact come to a standstill by the time they caught up. George put down the camera box with relief and stretched her arm.

'It's not much further,' Lukas said abruptly. 'You can rest when we get there. Mark! Give these girls a drink for God's sake!' He opened the bag he was carrying and handed him a few cans. George would have liked a drink, but suspected that the term 'girls' did not include her and she wasn't giving him the satisfaction of asking. Lukas was already moving on and George shouldered the camera case and scooted after him. Keeping on his good side professionally was more important than a drink right now. A quarter of an hour later, with George fit to drop from his punishing pace, they reached a pile of rocks in the river bed around which a stream ran like a moat.

George had a dry mouth and her lungs felt as if they would burst from breathing air that seemed to get hotter with every lungful. She thought longingly of the drinks given to the girls and hoped there would be something for the workers.

'It's a bit like trying to work in a sauna, isn't it?' Lukas remarked.

George smiled a little wanly. 'I wouldn't know. I've never tried.'

'I have. It's difficult. The lenses keep steaming up.'

'So why do you waste your time on this rubbish, Lukas?'

He looked up, suddenly angry. 'Some of us have rent to pay,' he said curtly. 'And you're here. What's your excuse?'

She blinked, furious with herself. She just wasn't used to keeping her feelings to herself. Perhaps it was time she learned. 'You'll want the camera about here,' she said, changing the subject.

'It'll do for a start.'

George turned to set up the tripod and froze, feeling the blood drain from her face as she spotted a green lizard regarding her from the shadow of a pile of stones. As she stared it darted into the shadows.

Amber, discussing the shot with Lukas, caught the sudden movement. 'A snake!' she cried. 'I saw a snake!' She clung to him.

'It was only a lizard,' George said, trying to repress a shudder.

'No!' Amber was near hysteria. 'I saw it. It's under the rock!'

'Get it out, George, there's a good girl. I've got my hands full.' She looked up at him, not believing her ears. 'Or we won't get anything done today.'

He had thrown down a challenge, daring her to refuse. She swallowed, but her throat was dry, and she wiped her hands on the seat of her trousers. Then slowly she bent down and stared into the shadow under the rock. The lizard stared back. She made a sudden lunge and caught something under her hand. She hung on to it and staggered to her feet.

'Here.' She thrust it blindly at Lukas.

'All right, Amber? See, it was a lizard.

It got away, but left George its tail.'

'Poor little thing,' Amber murmured and wandered away.

George caught Lukas staring at her with something like admiration. It was a look that made her tremble in a way that no lizard could. She widened her mouth into a self-mocking little smile, and without any warning he smiled back. Quickly she dropped her head to the tripod, but her fingers weren't quite steady as she tightened a nut. Her heart was beating painfully fast and although she would have liked to put it down to the exertion she knew she would be kidding herself.

'I hope you'll be able to undo those,' Lukas broke into her thoughts, making her jump once more. 'Here, have a drink.' He handed her a can.

'Thank you.' She took it gratefully, and tipped the cold liquid down her throat.

'You need to keep topped up. This is a bad time of day to start work.' He took the can from her. 'If you're finished, we'll take some Polaroids.'

'I'll get the film.'

Mark looked up from laying out his colours in the lid of the make-up box.

'Sorry to bother you, but I need the film bag,' she asked.

'Film bag?'

'You carried it for me,' she prompted.

'Oh, that. I carried it for a while.' He thought for a moment. 'When we stopped for a drink I put it down. You took it from there,' he said carelessly.

George froze. 'No, Mark, I didn't stop.'

'Didn't you?' He shifted uncomfortably. 'Sorry, George. I'd go back for you, but I have to get on with the make-up.'

George felt cold. Standing in the blazing African heat, she shivered. 'Of course. You get on with what you're doing. I'll find it.'

She spent a few moments looking around before facing the inevitable explosion. Out of the corner of her eye she could see Lukas watching her.

Waiting impatiently. There was no point in putting the moment off. The bag had been left back on the river bed. And she was going to have to face him.

As she walked across the hot space, she knew how prisoners going to the scaffold must have felt. An inevitable, unavoidable fate was awaiting her.

'Well? Where's the film?'

She drew a deep breath. 'Back there, somewhere. Where the girls stopped for a drink.'

'I see.' Those two small words told her very plainly that she was an incompetent fool, but that he had never expected anything better. She flushed with humiliation.

'I'm sorry.'

'I'm sure you are. But not as sorry as you're going to be,' he warned. 'Meanwhile, you'd better do something about the film so that we can get some work done today.' With that, he turned and walked to the shade where he sat down, leaned back against a tree, and closed his eyes.

George dragged her eyes from him and stared back along the river bed for a moment, conscious of the sudden silence that had descended upon the group. Then, head high, she started to walk briskly back in the direction from which they had come.

She didn't slow, or shift her head to left or right, until a bend in the river hid her from their view. Then and only then did she pull a handkerchief from her trouser pocket and blow her nose. A group of vultures, nightmare creatures with bare heads and hunched shoulders, flapped awkwardly from a thicket of trees at this disturbance.

She took to her heels and ran, furious with Mark, with Lukas, but most of all herself for getting into such a mess. She should never have let the wretched bag out of her hand. She sank finally, on to her knees, breathing heavily, her heart thumping, her shirt sticking to her clammily. She didn't think she had ever felt so wretched in her life.

How could she have been so stupid? She sat back on her heels and pounded her fist against her knee in frustration. She knew that one day she would laugh at the ridiculous spectacle she was making of herself. But not now. Instead she took off the horrible hat and dipped it into a pool, and, trying not to think about what might be in the water, she dumped it back on her head. Then she started to hunt for the bag.

She didn't have to look for long. It was in the shade of a rock, easily forgotten by someone whose life did not depend upon it. She picked it up and began the hot walk back to face Lukas.

It seemed forever before she turned the bend in the river and saw them. Lukas and Walter, deep in discussion, turned as she approached.

She went straight to the camera and replaced its back with one she had previously loaded with Polaroid film.

'You'd better have a drink, George,' Walter suggested.

'Later,' Lukas snapped, brushing him aside. 'We've wasted enough time.'

Kelly rose majestically from the rug where she had been sitting cross-legged, draped in a light cotton wrap. She shrugged it off to reveal the native fabric draped about her hips and a magnificent choker threaded from the tiny nuts and cogs. She walked with an arrow-straight back to the rock. As she lay back upon it Suzy whisked away her sandals and left her, like Andromeda, to await her fate at the jaws of some imaginary dragon. Lukas, staring through the camera, called out instructions to her, taking Polaroids and passing them to George to peel them free of their backings.

After that everything just became a blur as she constantly checked light, held reflectors, replaced film, film and more film.

Finally Lukas was satisfied and Kelly climbed down. 'That rock is hard,' was all the comment she made as she walked stiffly back to her rug. George found herself admiring the girl's professionalism. There was a lack of nonsense about the way she had done exactly what was wanted, in uncomfortable circumstances, with the absolute minimum of fuss.

'That's a tough way to make a living,' she said, as she packed the exposed film back into the cold bag.

'Is there an easy way?' Kelly asked, yawning. 'Oh, God, this sun is so tiring.'

'Yes,' George agreed, pulling a face, suddenly conscious of a thumping headache and a pain behind her eyes from the sun.

Kelly looked concerned. 'Are you all right? Here, have a swig of this, you must be parched.'

Gratefully George took the proffered can. It wasn't very cold, but it was wet and she was grateful. 'So,' she asked, 'what next?'

'We go back to camp,' Lukas said, coming up behind them. 'Some of us have earned a rest.' He picked up the cold box and turned away.

'I'll carry that,' George said. 'It's my job.'

He turned and regarded her steadily. 'A pity you didn't think of that earlier.'

'I shan't make the same mistake again. Please leave it to me.' She tried to keep the pleading out of her voice, but it was a matter of pride. He dropped the box at her feet.

'If you're sure. I wouldn't want to put you to any trouble.'

'Quite sure.' Her voice wasn't quite steady, as he held her for a moment in his gaze. Then he shrugged and walked away.

'Whew!' Kelly said, with feeling. 'Who's rattled his cage?'

'I'll give you three guesses,' George murmured. She emptied the can, and threw it back into the box.

'Come on,' Kelly said. 'I'll give you a hand.'

George smiled, truly grateful for the girl's offer. 'I think perhaps I'd better do my penance to the bitter end, don't you?' she said, lightly. 'But thanks. I appreciate the offer.'

Lukas was strolling away with Walter as George dismantled the tripod and packed it away in its case. It had the bulk and weight of a small set of golf clubs. Lukas had carried it from the jeep but while she had been working he and Walter had disappeared. The camera had already been packed by Lukas. George, not to be caught out twice in one day, checked that it was all there. Satisfied, she gathered her equipment and with the tripod over her shoulder and a bag in each hand she began a slow trudge back to the jeep, not even attempting to catch up with the others.

By the time the jeep appeared above her, with Lukas and Walter sitting comfortably in camp chairs under the trees, George was beyond feeling. The bank loomed ahead of her and she knew she wasn't going to make it. And she didn't care.

She understood vaguely that the bags

had been taken from her, that the weight had gone from her shoulders, but that made no difference. Her legs were jelly, and spots were converging before her eyes. She wondered, without much interest, if they would leave her behind.

'George!' Lukas sounded a long way away. 'George, are you all right?' But that couldn't be right because his arms were around her. As he lifted her, her hat fell off. Her last thought, before everything went dark, was that she mustn't lose her hat.

# 4

'George! George!' The voice was urgent and George knew that she really ought to do something about it. 'She's coming round. For heaven's sake give her some air, everyone.' George made a supreme effort and opened her eyes. For a moment she was quite content to lie there. Then Lukas swam into focus and with him the remembrance of the last disastrous twenty-four hours. She tried to sit up, but his hand on her shoulder restrained her.

'Just keep still for a minute. Here, try a sip of this.' He pressed a can of something cold against her lips and she gulped as the liquid fizzed into her mouth, then struggled up, coughing and spluttering and gasping for air.

'God give me strength!' George found herself hauled unceremoniously over his shoulder and her back slapped sharply. The coughing stopped. She leaned weakly against him, her head resting upon his shoulder, his arm around her, holding her close against his chest. For a moment she was content to rest there while she willed her limbs into some sort of life. 'Better?' he demanded. She would have laughed if she had had the strength.

When she didn't answer he turned and looked at her, concerned grey eyes so close that for a moment she was mesmerised by them. Then a small frown creased his forehead and George remembered with a start exactly where she was. The speculative look that had sharpened his gaze was more reviving than any amount of first aid.

She tried a smile. 'Wonderful,' she said faintly. 'A slight case of sunstroke, a lungful of lemonade and a bruised back. Apart from that I feel . . . ' she waved vaguely ' . . . just wonderful. You should try it some time.' She lifted arms like lead and reluctantly pushed herself away from the comfort of his arms and on to legs still not entirely ready to carry her. She brushed a strand of hair from her face and with a sinking feeling she realised that she had lost the protection of her glasses. She glanced around, wondering where they had fallen.

Lukas, with a sardonic expression, produced them from his jacket pocket. 'They're quite safe,' he said, and produced a handkerchief with which to polish them, holding them up to the light and peering carefully through them to make sure they were clean. 'These were what you were looking for, I imagine?' He was standing very close as he slipped them on to her nose and with a thoughtful expression he brushed back a wayward strand of hair and tucked it behind her ear. 'I know you can't manage without them.' His smile was pure mockery.

George stepped back quickly and pushed the spectacles firmly up her nose. More confident behind her screen, she looked around for her hat. It was still down on the river bed.

Lukas followed her glance and sighed. 'I had hoped you would be able to manage without that,' he murmured. 'Get the lady's hat, Mark. Then perhaps we can get back to camp without any more disasters befalling us.' He took George's arm and led her firmly to the front of the jeep. 'Up you get.'

'I'll get in the back,' she protested, but Lukas shook his head. 'Oh, no, my dear. If you feel sick, I should prefer it if you had a window handy.'

'I won't . . . ' He didn't bother to argue. Instead she was scooped up and dumped on to the front seat. Her head was thumping too painfully for her to protest further and she slumped against the unyielding seat and closed her eyes. She immediately opened them again in panic. 'The camera . . . ?'

'Is fine. It's already packed away.' Lukas allowed himself a small smile. 'I caught it before you managed to — er — *drop* it.' He closed the door firmly on her.

A little desultory conversation in the back filtered into George's head as they drove back to camp, but Lukas was silent and brooding beside her and she wondered if he was planning to dispatch her back to Nairobi without delay. She had hardly acquitted herself with glory and had given him more than sufficient cause to rid himself of her. In fact she had been a total disaster as his assistant, and she couldn't find it in her heart to blame him. Suddenly her throat ached with unshed tears for her refuge, and the homeless ones who would have benefited from it. She had failed them. Damn Lukas. And damn Pa . . .

'The window is on your left.' George stared uncomprehendingly at Lukas. 'You looked a bit green. I just wanted to be sure you knew where the window was.'

'Green?' George managed a careless laugh. 'That's just my sun-block.'

The jeep bounced into camp and Lukas parked it in the shade of a tree.

George didn't wait to be helped down, but opened the door and jumped. For a second her knees buckled, but pride determined that he shouldn't see how weak she felt. She opened the rear door and unloaded the bags, then reached for the tripod. Lukas leaned across and took it from her.

'I usually carry the tripod. I shouldn't have left it back there for you,' he addressed the air somewhere over her head. 'If I do it again, just leave it. It would serve me right if I had to go back for it.'

It was probably as near to an apology as she would ever get and they both knew it. 'Whatever you say,' she said with a sudden lifting of her heart as she realised he was saying that she could stay. 'Boss,' she added, with the slightest twinkle.

She heard Walter chuckle behind her. 'Is something amusing you, Walter?' Lukas demanded.

'No. Nothing.' He glanced at George and chuckled again. 'Boss.'

Lukas caught her arm and pulled her away from the jeep. 'Come on. Let's get this film sorted out. Then Walter can drive up to Nairobi with it. We'll see if he thinks that's so funny.'

She had to half run to keep up with his long strides. 'Do you send film after each day's shoot?' she asked, breathlessly, as they arrived at the store tent. 'That must be very expensive.'

His look was scathing. 'Worrying about Daddy's money? Is that the reason you dress in jumble-sale remnants?' His look was scathing as his eyes swept over her. 'It would be a bit of a blow to look at the slides when I get back to England and find that I'd chopped all the girls' heads off.'

She replaced the unused film in the refrigerator, taking her time, making the most of the welcome blast of cold air. 'Do you think anyone would notice?' she snapped, irritated by his comment about her clothes.

He glared at her. 'Very funny. Come on. I'll give this to Walter and we can have a cup of tea.' He held out his hand and after the slightest hesitation she took it, allowing him to pull her to her feet. For a moment he surveyed her critically, until she found herself flushing under the intensity of his gaze. 'You're looking better, George. Tell me, do you always go about dressed like an advert for a church jumble sale?'

George knew it was ridiculous to feel peeved by his remarks. After all, she had brought it on herself. But a small part of her found it galling, would have liked to see that expression in his eyes that had so enraged her when their paths had crossed before. But, with the tiniest regret, she managed to fix a huge smile to her mouth and launched herself back into character.

'Oh, absolutely! I do believe in recycling, don't you?' she asked him earnestly. 'After all, if these clothes were thrown away they would just fill up some hole in the ground until they rotted and started to produce methane . . . ' She managed to retrieve her hand and began to walk to the mess tent.

'Have you ever considered that methane might be the lesser of two evils?' he persisted.

'Come on, Lukas. You're not that thick. You must know as well as I do about the problem of global warming. I had to spend a lot of time persuading Pa about the benefits of recycling, but even he eventually saw the light. He recycles all the waste paper from his offices, uses low-energy lighting, there's so much that can be done — '

'All right!' Lukas stepped in front of her and George was forced to a halt. 'I promise I won't make any more comments about your clothes on one condition.'

'Oh? And what's that?'

'Abandon that bloody awful hat.'

George's smile reached her eyes as she pulled her hat more firmly on her head. 'Oh, that's all right, Lukas. Make all the comments you want, I don't mind a bit. The more people I can convince the better.'

'God, but you're stubborn!' He leaned towards her.

She didn't flinch. 'So are you!' They glared at each other for a long moment, and Lukas welcomed Walter's intervention with apparent relief.

'Here are the films. Will Mark be all right driving the other jeep back?'

'No problem. I'll pick up the post and the newspapers from the Norfolk as well.'

George's hand shook as she poured the tea. Newspapers?

'Are you still feeling shaky, George?' Kelly asked, with concern. 'Here, let me do that.' Kelly poured the tea and handed them each a cup.

'Sorry. I'm just a bit tired,' George excused herself, as she considered the implication of what she had heard.

'Not too tired to come and look at tomorrow's set, I hope,' Lukas challenged her over the edge of his teacup.

George tried to hide her dismay. It was a real effort to concentrate on being a thick-skinned dimwit under that slightly disbelieving stare. 'No. Of course not. Where are we going?'

'There's a village a few miles upstream. We're using it for Amber's 'white African queen' shot. I'll want you to go over early tomorrow and set it up.' He paused. 'If you think you can manage it.'

'I'll do my best,' George replied evenly.

'Exactly my meaning.'

She resisted the urge to throw her tea, cup and all, at him and stood up.

'If you can just spare me a few minutes to freshen up?'

'Just a few.'

The tent was hot and airless and George had no desire to stay there longer than necessary. She stripped off and washed as quickly as she could, nervous that Lukas might suddenly appear.

The examination of the contents of her bag revealed a pair of khaki Bermuda shorts that looked comfortable and she added a man's white shirt to hang baggily over them. Without a mirror it was difficult to tell exactly what the effect was, but George hoped that she had retained the air of a refugee from a charity shop.

She brushed out her hair, enjoying briefly the feeling of freedom from hat and hairpins.

'Are you decent?' Lukas enquired, his voice just outside the tent. He didn't wait for her answer.

In a sudden panic George gathered her hair as the flap lifted and sunlight flooded the tent. She twisted it up and attempted to skewer the resulting knot with her hairpins.

'For heaven's sake stop titivating and let's get going. I don't want to be driving about the bush after dark unless I have to.'

George's hand trembled, the pins slipped and her hair descended around her shoulders. 'Dark? But it's only half-past four.'

There was a sudden stillness about

Lukas and he regarded her steadily. 'It'll be dark by six. We're almost on the equator here.' He took a handful of her hair and allowed it to slide between his fingers. 'Lovely. Like evening sunshine. Why do you hide it in a bun?'

George regained control of the pins and turned abruptly away from him. 'It gets in the way.' She swept it up into a twist and deftly pinned it into place. Then she replaced her glasses and picked up her hat and jammed it on her head.

She hung her camera around her neck and followed Lukas to the jeep. He opened the door for her with a flourish.

'I don't suppose you opened doors for Michael,' she said with irritation. 'I don't expect any concessions, you know. You can treat me exactly the same.'

'As Michael?' He appeared to be amused by this suggestion.

'Yes. Your last assistant. The young man in hospital.'

'That would be difficult.' He smiled lazily down at her. 'Michael didn't have quite the same effect on me as you do, George.' She felt the colour rise in her cheeks and her body reminded her with a jolt the feelings he had awoken in her before. 'I didn't have a constant and overwhelming urge to shake him.' George released the breath she had not been aware she was holding. 'Or do this.' His lips touched hers before she had time to side-step him. The kiss was the lightest exploration of the possibilities. He made no move to touch her, or restrain her, but before he raised his head her body was vibrating in response. Lukas stepped back and regarded her thoughtfully. 'It'll come to me,' he murmured. 'I never forget a face.' He indicated the interior of the jeep. 'Shall we go?'

George did not move. The sudden realisation that a sort of guerilla warfare had broken out between them had left her deeply apprehensive. She knew she had started it, but she had just lost control of the game and she didn't know what the rules were. If indeed there were any rules.

'Well?' His eyes were laughing at her and George scrambled up into the jeep with more haste than elegance. Lukas climbed in alongside her, apparently oblivious to her hot cheeks. He started the engine and the jeep began to bounce towards the track. He began to discuss the shoot as if nothing had happened between them. George shook herself mentally. Nothing must. She made an effort to regain a measure of control.

'Lukas?' He glanced across at her. 'About my being called George.'

'A very silly notion, in my opinion.'

George ignored this. 'I meant what I said just now. I expect you to treat me exactly as if I were Michael.' She was very firm.

'Except I should call you George,' he mocked.

She knew she was blushing, but she had to make the point. 'You know what I mean.'

'Oh, yes. I know what you mean.' A muscle tightened at the side of his mouth. 'I mustn't make passes at girls who wear glasses. Perhaps it would be as well. I don't suppose Daddy would approve. Will you tell him we're sharing a tent?'

'It's nothing to do with . . . ' She left the words unsaid. Maybe that would be the best way. 'No,' she said, with genuine embarrassment at the deception. 'I don't suppose he would approve at all.'

'Perhaps we could get back to work, then,' he suggested. 'Tomorrow morning I want you to bring over the props for the set and get it ready for us.' He glanced sideways at her. 'You can drive?'

'Yes, of course. You'll want me to come back for you when I've got everything ready?'

'No. Mark and Walter are bringing the other jeep back from Nairobi tonight, which is a relief. I don't like being down here without a spare vehicle.'

'So? Why are you?'

'Michael tried to write the other one off. However, he did himself more damage than the Land Rover.'

'Was he badly hurt?' George asked, concern driving out all other thoughts.

'Nothing that won't mend. In the meantime he can lie and meditate on the wisdom of drinking and driving. And thank his lucky stars it didn't happen in Britain where he would almost certainly have lost his licence.'

'Silly boy.'

Lukas grimaced. 'On that point, at least, we are in complete agreement. Here's the village.'

The village consisted of a number of circular huts built around a clearing. As the jeep drove in, smaller children dived for shelter behind mothers, while a group of boys with a pack of dogs chased the jeep into the clearing. George had her camera up and working before they stopped.

The older children gathered around Lukas as he climbed down, calling his name with enthusiasm. George watched with surprise as he allowed them to swarm over him, finally surrendering good-humouredly to their entreaties and producing a bag of mints from his pocket. She took great pleasure in snapping this unexpected side to his nature.

'Lukas.' She drew his attention to the little ones. He beckoned to them, but they shrank further behind their mothers' skirts, so he bent down, squatting on his heels, reducing his bulk to less daunting proportions. They came shyly then, clapped their hands together politely, grabbed a sweet each and ran back to safety.

An old man, dressed in clean but worn trousers and a vest that had seen many better days, came forward and greeted Lukas, who turned and beckoned to George. She scrambled inelegantly down, wishing, not for the first time, that she was taller.

'*Jambo, mzee*,' she greeted the old man politely and, the formalities over,

Lukas took her to show her where the set was to be built.

'Where are the tyres?' she asked.

'Walter's bringing them down from Nairobi tonight. We wanted to be sure of getting the right ones. The villagers are going to barter them afterwards for some concrete blocks to help build a school.'

'They're building a school? Here?' George asked with amazement.

'You find that so surprising?'

She ignored his acid tone. 'I'd love to see. Would they let me have a look, do you think?'

Lukas sighed. 'I'm sure they'd be delighted. But if you could just give me your attention for a moment.' He recalled her to business, explaining the layout of the set, drawing in the dust with a long stick the positions of the various props. She copied the plan into a notebook, carefully pacing out the distances. By the time she had finished Lukas had disappeared.

She found him sitting outside the

largest hut with the village elder who indicated that she should sit on his other side. She sank on to the mat and crossed her legs, glad that she wasn't wearing a skirt.

A girl appeared with three cups and poured a thick brown liquid from a blackened enamel teapot. George thanked her and stared down at the cup. She raised a questioning glance at Lukas, who, totally expressionless, picked up his cup and sipped. His eyes were a silent challenge for her to do the same, but George could feel her stomach rebelling at the thought of drinking the unknown brew from a chipped and rather grubby cup.

She recalled her grandmother telling her about some tea she had to drink in the Himalayas. It had been black, with rancid yak butter floating in it, and it had been covered in flies. Well, she had lived to tell the tale. Family honour was at stake. It would be something to tell her own grandchildren. Assuming that she was as lucky as her grandmother.

She sketched a smile and lifted the cup to her lips. Offering up a silent prayer, she sipped. It was tea, strong and unbearably sweet with precious sugar and evaporated milk. She raised her eyes over the brim of the cup. '*Mzuri, sana*,' she said appreciatively to the old man, who beamed with pleasure. 'It's very good.' Her large violet eyes met the sardonic challenge Lukas had thrown down and she sipped slowly and deliberately, having banished the cup, its contents, and the hard ground she was sitting on, from her mind. She was concentrating very hard on the fact that she was drinking China tea from the Minton set at home. It wasn't easy.

Lukas watched impassively as she finished every drop, then rose, and George, feeling decidedly queasy, followed his example.

She thanked the old man for his hospitality, and the girl, who giggled shyly, and, clutching her notebook tightly, walked carefully back to the jeep.

'A bravura performance, if I may say so,' Lukas grinned with apparent delight at her discomfort.

'Merely politeness,' George said stiffly, trying not to think about the bumpy track ahead. 'Can we go now?'

'But I thought you wanted to see the school,' he teased remorselessly.

'Tomorrow,' she said firmly. 'I'll look tomorrow.'

She was glad of his help into the jeep. 'A good idea. It wouldn't do to bring up their tea in front of them. Not at all the famous British good manners.' He started the engine. 'And I begin to suspect that you come from a long line of those formidable English ladies who tamed the natives with afternoon tea and the Church of England.'

She had the grace to smile. 'Well, the natives got their own back today.' She held on to her seat as the sweat broke out on her upper lip, wincing as they bounced out of a deep rut and she tasted bile in the back of her throat. 'Could we please change the subject?'

She held on to her stomach, and Lukas pulled up.

He reached behind him and produced a can of lemonade. 'Here. This will help. Just sip it.' She pulled the ring-pull and the drink erupted, cascading over him. He leapt back, swearing. 'I don't believe it!' he yelled. 'What kind of disaster are you?'

She was beyond caring what he thought. She sipped the drink and as soon as the taste of the tea had gone she began to feel better.

'I'm sorry about your shirt.' She finally managed an apology.

'So am I.' He glared at her, then threw up his hands in resignation. 'What is it about you that makes me react like a monster?'

'My natural sunny disposition?' she suggested. 'My charm?' She giggled. 'My dress sense?'

He shook his head. 'There's something . . . but never mind. Have you ever seen anything like that?'

George turned to look out of the

window. A huge red sun was disappearing behind the distant hills, and down in the river bed a group of giraffe were drinking at a pool.

'No. It's beautiful.'

'Mmm. Perfect.' He paused and considered her. 'Now, if you were not George at this moment, but Georgette, I would not be wasting such a very special moment.'

'Wasting? How could looking at all this be a waste?'

Lukas slid an arm along the seat behind her and smiled indulgently. 'You'd really like to know?'

'I don't think . . . ' Plainly it would be better not to pursue this line of thought, but he was not to be stopped.

'First, I should have to remove this horrible thing. So.' He plucked the hat from her head and threw it into the back of the jeep.

'Lukas!' she protested, backing hard against the jeep door.

'Next,' he smiled, 'always supposing you were Georgette, of course, I should remove these hairpins one by one.' His hands released her hair and it descended around her shoulders and glowed like fire in the light of the setting sun. He took a handful and, wrapping it around his fist, he drew her closer to him. 'I might even take the time to wonder why any woman should want to hide such glory.'

'Lukas! Stop this,' she begged, her treacherous body glowing as he teased her remorselessly, her lips parting in unconscious response to him. He removed her spectacles and regarded her steadily.

'And then . . . ' he continued as if she hadn't spoken. He touched her cheek and ran his thumb down her jaw, lifting her chin, turning her mouth to his. 'Then perhaps she would choose to distract me from all the odd little thoughts running through my brain.' George made a small sound in the back of her throat as his mouth, warm and mobile, descended upon hers. Then, even before she could protest, it was over. He smiled lazily down at her.

'But it's all academic. Because Georgette is George. And wishes to be treated exactly like Michael. And Michael,' he added with a mocking twist to his mouth, 'Michael would have flattened me if I had dared to take such liberties.'

'I doubt,' George said, as steadily as she could, 'I very much doubt that Michael wears hairpins.'

He grinned quite suddenly. 'You have a point there.'

He finally released her and leaned forward to start the engine. 'It is time to be getting back. They will be worrying about us.'

And with good reason, George thought, as she tried to control her wildly racing pulse. The man was loaded with a dangerous charm when he chose to exercise it, and she had gone more than halfway to meeting him. It simply wasn't fair that she found him so totally desirable, when she was almost certain that she didn't even like him. Crossly she scooped her hair up and searched for the pins that Lukas had dropped. But the floor of the jeep was dark and in the end she gave up and let her hair fall. Instead she took particular pleasure in retrieving her hat and jamming it firmly back on her head.

Lukas had put on the headlights and she realised quite suddenly how dark it had become. She gripped her seat nervously.

'Why did you come here to take your calendar shots?' she asked. Anything to distract her mind from the thought of the dark out there. 'Surely you could have chosen somewhere a lot safer.'

'Safer?' Lukas shrugged. 'I suppose so. But it's got to be a sort of silly tradition. MotorParts gets to the places other spares cannot reach. That sort of thing.' He glanced across at her. 'If you think this is tough you should have been in Finland.'

'Finland?' What was so awful about Finland? It was daylight nearly all the time there. Then she realised. 'You mean the girls . . . ? In the snow?'

'A few strategic furs, but basically, yes.' She saw the whiteness of his teeth in the darkness. 'It was tough on the girls. The goose-bumps were a real menace. I practically wore out my soft-focus filter.'

She bridled at the unspoken criticism. 'I suppose you think me very soft. I'm not normally inclined to fainting and sickness, Lukas, it's just been a rather long and trying day.'

'You're not soft, George. A lot of things, but not that. But every day here is going to be long and trying. Do you really want to stay?' He allowed the faintest hope to colour his voice.

'Umm?' George smothered a yawn. 'Oh, yes. I have to stay. I have no choice.'

# 5

'Why?'

There was a deceptive lightness about the question that put George immediately on her guard. She was letting her concentration slip. 'Why?' she queried, forcing another yawn in order to give herself time to think.

'Why do you have no choice?' Lukas's voice was even, but there was a dangerous edge to it.

'Oh! I see what you're getting at,' she said, with a soft laugh. 'It's Pa. He wants me to learn as much as I can working with you.' She concentrated on a look of earnest puzzlement. 'He thinks you're a very good photographer.'

'But you don't agree?' Amusement had reasserted itself, and there was an ironic twist to his mouth.

'Oh, no!' She frowned slightly. 'No,

that's wrong. What I mean is, yes. I do agree with him.' She looked at him gravely, her eyes wide with admiration. 'I think you're wonderful.'

'You'd do wonders for my ego, George, if it weren't for the fact that there's a great big 'but' in there somewhere.' His eyes gleamed in the gathering darkness, as he turned a thoughtful smile on her.

'Well, of course I'd much rather be taking a different kind of picture. Does my father actually know that his calendar is going to have all these girls on them?'

'I imagine it highly likely. We've been producing them for the last six years.' Lukas was clearly exasperated. 'You do realise that they are collectors' items, don't you? There is the most tremendous fuss every year to try and produce something original. Beautiful. That to receive one is considered a sign that you have *arrived* in the motor trade? These aren't the sort of thing you see on the walls of garage workshops, you know.'

George ignored this. 'I'm sure I could find a much more worthwhile theme,' she went on thoughtfully. 'Perhaps it's time to go 'green'. What do you think of *Endangered Species of the British Isles*?'

His straight black brows rose slightly. 'If you can get your father to agree I will naturally do my best. But,' he warned, 'I'll insist that you come along as well.'

'As your assistant?' George asked, with what she hoped sounded like rapture.

'No. I'll need you to *nag* the natterjack toads into behaving for the camera,' he snapped.

George spent the remainder of the journey in a warm little glow of satisfaction. But it only lasted until the lights of the camp appeared and Lukas drew up, pulling savagely on the handbrake. He opened his door, jumped down and walked away, leaving George to manage by herself.

She sat very still in the jeep. It was

safe there. The engine was making familiar, comforting ticking noises as it cooled. Not like the dark space between it and the lighted mess tent. But she had to make a move. The alternatives were shouting for help, and staying there all night, both equally unappealing. With a great effort of will she opened the door and gingerly climbed down. Nothing happened. No monster grabbed her. The only monster, she reminded herself, was in her own mind. She allowed her nerves to relax an inch or two. Then something rustled in the darkness at her feet and she took to her heels and ran.

She pulled up sharply as she reached the light, feeling foolish before the raised eyebrows of the group gathered there under the hissing of the portable gaslight.

'A drink, George?' Lukas asked, the smallest smile betraying his amusement. 'Something to steady your nerves?'

'A gin and tonic. Please.'

He poured her drink and placed it in her hand, pressing his fingers around hers, holding them firmly, teasing laughter creasing his eyes. When he was sure the glass was safe he turned to Walter. 'Did you bring the papers back from Nairobi?'

'Yes. But I left them in the jeep. And your laundry. We've only just got back. I'll fetch them.' He began to heave himself out of his chair.

'No, don't get up. George will be glad to fetch them for you. Won't you, George?' He rescued the glass as her fingers twitched.

Walter subsided with relief. 'That's right. Wear the young ones out first.'

George felt her mouth go dry as she looked into the blackness. It was so thick out there that she felt she would disappear into it if she left the friendly light of the tent, and never be seen again.

'I can't . . . ' She cleared her throat and tried again. 'I can't actually see the jeep. Where did you leave it?'

131

'Over there.' Walter indicated vaguely. 'Here, take my torch.'

'There. You'll be quite safe now.' Lukas raised his glass in a little salute. 'Off you go.'

She switched on the torch and a powerful beam leapt out into the darkness, picking out the Land Rover parked beneath a slender palm. Her heart was pounding high in her throat as she ran to the vehicle, and her fingers trembled on the door-handle as she wrenched it open. There was a parcel on the back seat, and a thick pile of newspapers. She climbed in to reach them.

The torchlight wavered as George glanced back at the tent. No one was watching her and Lukas was deep in conversation with Walter. She returned to the papers and, holding her breath, she flipped through them. Near the bottom she found the one she had hoped wouldn't be there. The one with her plastered over the front page. She pulled it out and glanced around for a hiding place. If she stuffed it behind the seat she could retrieve it in the morning. She put down the torch in order to roll the paper up and dispose of it. Satisfied that it was hidden from the casual observer, she reached out for the torch.

'Georgette Bainbridge! Where the hell are you? I want to get out of this wet shirt!' George jumped and swivelled guiltily on the seat, knocking the torch to the floor where it landed with a dull thud. Darkness descended, folding her suffocatingly in black cotton wool.

'Oh, God . . . ' she whimpered. 'Please . . . ' But God was busy elsewhere. Slowly she reached down, her flesh crawling with what she knew was an irrational fear. Gritting her teeth to stop herself from crying out, she began to feel about on the floor. Her hand knocked against the torch and with a little cry of relief she made a grab for it. Instead of the torch, her hand grasped something soft. George opened her mouth and screamed.

The door beside her jerked wide open. 'What on earth . . . ?'

Lukas was staring at her in astonishment. For a moment she was frozen, unable to move, then with a shuddering sob she threw herself out of the jeep and into his arms. 'There's something there,' she cried. 'I touched it.' She clung to him, burying her head in his shoulder, frantic for the safety he represented. She could feel the steady beating of his heart as he held her close against his broad chest, and gradually sanity began to return and with it some recognition of where she was. She tried to pull away but her rescuer was now her captor.

'Well, Georgette . . . ' Lukas said softly.

'No . . . !' She looked up to see a mocking little smile playing about his mouth.

'Oh, yes, my dear. You should have found out a little bit about Michael before you insisted upon being treated like him.' He looked over her head into the jeep. 'You see, as well as being an excellent photographer, Michael is an entomologist. That's why he came with me on this shoot. If he had encountered something strange in the dark I can assure you he wouldn't have screamed. He would have popped it into one of the little bottles he carried about his person.' He gripped her shoulders. 'Although frankly, I believe that this specimen might have defeated even him. Now, Georgette, I think it would be best if you confronted the beast that reduced you to this — er — state.'

'No!'

Firmly, oblivious to her efforts to resist, he propelled her around to face her fear. George averted her face and kept her eyes tight shut.

'Look at it,' Lukas commanded. 'It won't hurt you. Trust me.'

'I . . . can't.'

'Trust me,' he repeated, and slowly George did as she was told. For a moment what she was seeing didn't register and she drew her well-defined brows into a puzzled frown.

'My hat?' Involuntarily she lifted her hand to her head. It must have fallen off when Lukas had startled her.

'Your hat, Georgette.' There was no mistaking the relish in his voice. 'Perhaps you will believe me now when I tell you that it is a fright. In fact, a nightmare of a hat.' He grinned. 'And, if it's not too much trouble, I should like my laundry now.'

'Your laundry?' She picked up the package from the seat. 'This laundry?'

'That's right. You can bring it to my — correction, *our* tent.' He turned on his heel and walked away. George hefted the parcel to shoulder height and hurled it after him. It missed him by inches. He laughed softly.

'Ohhh!'

Furiously she grabbed the torch, hat and newspapers. There was a sudden roar of noise. George just managed to hold on to the torch as she jumped again. Light flickered across the compound as a generator caught uncertainly and then brightened as it settled to a steady rhythm. She stood still until her heart had returned to something nearer its normal pace, but with the banishment of the dark her spirits suddenly lifted.

'Stupid girl,' she admonished herself as she retrieved the parcel of laundry and hurried across to the tent where Lukas was waiting.

'All right?' he enquired.

'Never better,' she affirmed stoutly.

'So you'll be staying?' He retrieved the parcel from her arms and threw it on to his bed.

'Don't worry, Lukas. I won't leave you to manage by yourself,' she reassured him soothingly. 'And you must think of your reputation. To lose one assistant might be considered a misfortune. To lose two must surely be thought carelessness.'

He took a step towards her, and she backed hastily. Lukas smiled, fully aware of the effect he was having on her. 'You'd better have these back, then, hadn't you?' He produced her glasses from his pocket and opened them as a preliminary to placing them on her nose. She plucked them from his hand and pushed them firmly into her own pocket.

He grinned. 'Spoil-sport. And if it had been a big hairy spider in the Land Rover?'

George crossed her fingers. 'I'm not afraid of spiders,' she lied desperately. She wasn't handing him a weapon like that to use against her. 'It was just the dark.'

'The dark?' He seemed genuinely surprised. 'You're afraid of the dark? I thought it was creepy crawlies that were putting the wind up you.'

'I know it's silly.'

'Yes. Very silly. The dark is beautiful, George. Come on, I'll show you.' He caught her hand.

'No. You want to change . . . '

'Later. Come on.' He led her to the tent entrance and paused there, looking down at her. 'I'll keep you quite safe. I promise.'

She looked up into his eyes and saw with surprise that he was no longer teasing her, and she allowed him to lead her outside, away from the camp site and into the complete darkness of the bush. There were small noises about them, rustlings from unseen creatures that made her skin prickle. He seemed to sense her unease.

'Stand still.'

'No. Lukas, I can't. Take me back,' she whimpered.

'Keep still,' he insisted. 'Open your eyes.'

She hadn't realised that they were closed, screwed up tight against unnameable fears. 'Oh!' He chuckled at her surprise. 'It's not really dark at all.'

'No. Of course it isn't. The starlight here is bright enough to see by.' Away from all man-made lights the heavens were thick with stars. 'There.' He pointed. 'Do you see the Southern Cross?'

'The lop-sided one?'

'Well, I've heard it described with

more enthusiasm, but yes.'

'Thank you for showing me.'

'My pleasure. But I think that's enough for tonight. If you don't put something on your legs, you'll be eaten alive by the mosquitoes.'

He led her back to the camp and held open the tent flap for her. She sank on to the camp bed, and a yawn, this time quite genuine, caught her by surprise.

* * *

'*Memsahib! Memsahib!*' An urgent voice woke her. '*Chai, memsahib*, for *bwana.*'

George forced heavy lids to open and saw the figure leaning over her. She sat up in a panic and then subsided as she remembered where she was.

'*Jambo, memsahib. Chai.*'

Seeing that she was awake, the steward placed the tray on the table and departed.

'Thank you,' she called belatedly, as

she swung her feet to the ground and searched for her sandals. She looked at her watch, but it was too dark to read the time.

'It's five o'clock.' His voice, out of the darkness, made her start. 'I hope you slept well.'

'I'll let you know,' she told the disembodied voice, 'in the morning.'

She heard him move on the other side of the tent and in the sudden flare of a lighted match saw a dark tousled head and bare chest unexpectedly close in the confines of the tent. She could have put out a hand and touched him. Just for a moment she considered doing exactly that. Their eyes met and he held hers in a mocking little smile, aware of her inspection. She blushed and looked away as the gaslight caught and hissed fiercely, bathing the tent in a harsh white light.

She busied herself pouring two cups and lifted one towards him as Lukas threw back the sheet and stood up. She found herself gazing somewhere in the region of a lean stomach that tapered to narrow hips. She jerked her eyes away and he laughed softly as he disappeared into the wash tent. The cup shook in its saucer and she quickly placed it on the table and covered her hot cheeks with her hands.

When Lukas reappeared he had a towel wrapped around him, to George's relief, and a scrap of tissue covering a cut on his chin.

His eyes met hers and he pulled a face. 'A bit tricky, shaving by torch-light.'

'Why on earth didn't you take the lamp?'

'I didn't want to leave you in the dark,' he said simply. 'You've only had lesson one.'

'Thank you.' She knew her fear was irrational and felt she owed him some explanation. 'I do know it's silly, but a cousin once shut me in a coal cellar . . . ' She shuddered, because even though that long, black hour had been years ago it still had the power to turn her into a gibbering wreck if she dwelt upon it.

'Charming cousin.'

George shrugged. 'He's a respected banker now. A pillar of society.'

'I hope he's not looking after my overdraft. I hate to think what he does with defaulters.'

'He's a bit grand for that sort of thing. I'm sure you're quite safe. I'd better get dressed.' She glanced down at her silk pyjamas. They were perfectly respectable, and yet seemed far too little covering, confined as she was in such close proximity to Lukas. 'You know, I was so tired last night, I don't even remember going to bed.'

'Really?' Lukas's eyes twinkled disturbingly as he held the tent flap for her and, clutching the torch and her clothes, she scurried through, taking great care not to brush against his naked chest.

Lukas was alone when she arrived at the mess tent. He waved his hand at the table. 'Help yourself. Kubwa will bring you eggs and bacon in a minute.'

'Good. I'm starving.'

He threw her an amused glance over his newspaper. 'I'm not surprised. You missed dinner. There's coffee over there. I'll have one too.' George poured two cups and passed one to him.

'Did Michael wait on you like this?' she asked.

'Michael would have been crawling about on the floor looking for bugs,' he replied from the depths of *The Times*. 'I'm beginning to think that in many ways, George, you're a great improvement on Michael. At least you don't snore.'

She felt herself colouring at this reminder of their enforced intimacy and covered her embarrassment in the task of pouring him coffee and then helped herself to a slice of fresh pineapple. By the time she had finished, the steward had appeared with two plates piled with bacon and eggs and some fresh toast.

'If you'll take the Land Rover this

morning you'll find it's already loaded up with the tyres. I'll just get the rest of the props for you.'

'What about the camera equipment?'

'I'll see to that and bring it with me.' He looked up from his breakfast. 'I want to set up a shot here for later. Michael's accident delayed us rather and the girls are booked for other jobs.'

'I'll do my best.'

'I'm not interested in your best. Just get it right.'

She rose from the table, controlling with great difficulty the urge to slap him. 'Yes, boss,' she murmured. 'If you'll point me in the right direction,' she added and then pulled up short at the sight that met her eyes. Dawn had come so gradually that inside the mess tent she hadn't noticed.

'The blessed daylight returns,' Lukas said behind her.

'It's beautiful,' George breathed, for once failing to rise to his irony.

Lukas followed her gaze. 'Yes. I suppose it is. But it's cool now. By mid-afternoon you'll be wishing the sun to blazes.'

* ★ ★

It didn't take that long. Piling up tyres to make a throne for Amber — She Who Must Be Obeyed — at any time of the day under an African sun was not George's idea of relaxation. Despite the early hour she was sweating from her exertions and she knew, without the benefit of a mirror, that she had smeared the oily grime from the tyres on to her face. She had broken one fingernail and was sure that she would lose several more before she had finished the job to her satisfaction. She pulled a face. Rather, to the satisfaction of Lukas. At least she hadn't got him breathing down her neck, making sly comments about her appearance. Or anything else that took his fancy.

She hauled another tyre into place with unnecessary force and it bounced playfully away. A soft giggle halted her mid-expletive and she turned to surprise a small girl watching her from behind a tree. '*Jambo, toto*,' she said, smiling and, following Lukas's example, she fished in her pocket for a packet of sweets that she had bought at the airport, but never opened.

The child took one, then clambered aboard the half-built throne. 'All right, princess,' George laughed. 'Stay right there.'

She had been awake enough to remember to bring her own camera equipment with her, and now fitted her favourite zoom lens and loaded a film. The child stared at it with interest from her high perch, but when George pointed it at her she began to wriggle down in panic.

Quickly George produced another sweet. The child hesitated, but with much encouragement finally settled down. Within a minute George found herself crowded by models eager to pose for this reward.

'*Kwisha*,' she said at last, showing

them the empty bag and then her empty pocket. The gesture was clear enough. No more sweets. Most of them drifted away, but her first friend had collected the wayward tyre and was waiting with it.

'*Asante, toto,*' George thanked her and the child smiled before running off to join the others.

George returned to her task, renewing her efforts to control the heavy tyres, until the throne matched the sketch she had been given. She fetched the box of spares from the Land Rover and a skin rug, which she laid in front of the throne.

Hot and thirsty, she leaned against the Land Rover and snapped open a cold drink. No one could say she wasn't a fast learner. She wouldn't be relying on anybody else to make sure she had enough to drink today.

As she sipped, a group of youths began clowning for her benefit, gesturing that she should come and take a picture of them, too. Laughing, she

148

turned her camera on them and focused, but it was Lukas who grinned down her lens. The boys had scattered.

'I assume everything is set up,' he said, walking towards her and taking the camera from her hands, 'as you have the time for a little freelance work.' He put it to his eye and turned slowly though an arc, surveying the village, until it came to rest on her. He pressed the shutter release and the motor wind whirred. Crossly George reached for her camera.

'I've no wish to be one of your pin-ups, Mr Lukas,' she snapped.

'Who's asking, sweetheart?' One dark brow arched in query, and George flushed, mortified at the unexpected surge of temper that had led her into making such an idiot of herself. It had been a simple snapshot, nothing more. She swallowed, hard.

'Don't you want to look at the set?'

'That's what I'm here for. Lead the way.' He stood back to allow her to pass and George walked stiffly to the result of all her hard work. 'Looks about right,' he conceded, giving the structure a kick. It held firm and Lukas nodded. 'I suppose it'll do.'

'It'll do! I've sweated blood . . . ' Too late she saw his smile. George began to assemble the hated tripod that seemed to have a life of its own, most of it spent trying to trap her fingers. It would help if they would just stop shaking.

'Hop up, George, will you?' Lukas pointed to the tyre throne. 'I want to check the light.'

'Me?' She straightened sharply. 'Couldn't Peach do it?'

'She'll get her clothes dirty on the tyres. Yours are beyond worrying about. Besides, you're the right colouring. Come on, up you get, there's a good girl.' She fought back an acid comment as she saw Peach watching her with amusement. She was dressed in an exquisite pale peach T-shirt, and tailored cream trousers, and looked as if she had just stepped out of a limousine. She seemed to repel dust and dirt.

George climbed up without further argument and perched primly on the throne she had worked so hard to build, keeping her eyes firmly on Mark as he began to paint Amber. Lukas was not fooled by her careful avoidance of his eye only inches from her own. 'Mark would paint you, if you asked nicely,' his voice caressed her like velvet.

She lowered her lids and glanced sideways at him. 'No. Thank you.'

'He'd make a better job of it than you at any rate.' His thumb grazed the streak of oil across her cheek. 'I'm not sure which I prefer, the green warpaint on your nose, or the oil.' She rubbed at it furiously with the sleeve of her shirt. Lukas grinned. 'Just stay there.' He went back to the camera and focused on her.

'You look quite at home up there, George,' Walter called out teasingly.

Contenting herself with a quelling glare at Lukas, she replied lightly, 'Oh, I am. Just ask Lukas. All I lack is a teapot and a parasol.'

Walter raised a questioning eyebrow at Lukas, whose expression did not alter as he concentrated upon the camera. But she was near enough to see his mouth twitch and the flicker of laughter deep in his eyes.

'What about your bible, Georgette?' he asked softly, so that only she could hear.

'It's in my bustle,' she hissed, and he gave a shout of laughter that drew six pairs of eyes in their direction.

'What's the joke?' Amber asked.

'It's nothing,' Lukas spluttered. 'It wouldn't translate.'

'Try us, dear boy,' encouraged Walter.

'It was just something about missionaries . . . ' His voice trailed away as he saw Walter smirk. 'Mark! Is that going to take all day?'

'Nearly finished, boss,' he called. 'I know a joke about a missionary . . . '

'We don't want to hear it,' Lukas snapped.

'Please yourself. There, all done, duchess.' Suzy inspected Mark's handiwork and, apparently satisfied, tied a skin cloth around the girl's hips and placed a dramatic shock-absorber pendant over her head on which the legend 'MotorPart' was clearly stamped.

After all the preparation, the actual photograph session was brief, and they were soon packed away. Walter, Mark and the models clambered back into the jeep, leaving Lukas and George alone.

'*Kwisha, bwana?*' the village elder asked.

'*Kwisha kabisa, mzee,*' Lukas affirmed. 'The tyres are all yours.' He indicated George. 'The *memsahib* would like to see this school you are building,' Lukas told him and the old man plucked at her sleeve with bony fingers.

'Come, come.' George threw a questioning glance at Lukas, surprised that he had remembered. His smile told her that he knew exactly what she was thinking and with a broad gesture he invited her to follow the old man.

'*Harambee!*' the old man said with a

great flourish, indicating a concrete foundation. '*Harambee* school!'

Lukas obliged. 'The local people raise the money. No government help.' The old man rattled away in Swahili and he translated for her. 'Mzee says that the tyres will buy enough blocks to build the school this high.' He held his hand against her waist and grinned. 'He wants to know if you would like to come on Sunday morning to help with the building.'

George was delighted with the invitation. 'Can we come?' she asked, hopefully.

'I had planned to drive to Nairobi, read the Sunday papers over a leisurely lunch, and spend the afternoon at the races.' He shrugged. 'But if you'd rather do this . . . '

'You can have a leisurely lunch any old Sunday. This will be fun,' she encouraged.

'Really? Do you promise?'

'Be serious!'

'Oh, I am being serious. I promise

you. And what about my Sunday lunch? It's Cook's day off.'

'You could cook it yourself,' George pointed out.

'I could,' he agreed. 'But I'm not going to. I've never yet had to cook for myself and I don't intend to start now.'

'Chauvinist pig,' George muttered under her breath, wondering why she was surprised. 'Oh, for heaven's sake. I'll see you get some lunch.'

'Roast beef?' he enquired, delicately. 'Yorkshire pudding?'

George threw a glance heavenwards. 'Whatever you say.'

Lukas smiled in satisfaction. 'In that case who am I to deny you the pleasure of laying concrete blocks on your day off? Perhaps one day you'll tell me what you do for fun? Dig latrines for Boy Scouts, perhaps?' He nodded to the old man. 'We'd be delighted to come. Now, George. Drive me home.' George stared in surprise, to the apparent satisfaction of Lukas. 'I am not, despite everything you believe about me, a chauvinist

— pig or otherwise. I am making an effort to prove it.' He grinned. 'Don't make me wish I hadn't.'

George tilted her head and regarded him with interest. 'I don't actually believe you, Lukas, but I'll be happy to drive.' She climbed into the driving seat, started the engine and engaged the gear. Glancing at him from under thick dark lashes, she released the clutch with extreme care. The Land Rover shot forward and stalled.

'Oops, sorry. Wrong gear.' She glanced at Lukas, whose expression remained passive. George found neutral and re-started the engine. Once more she selected a gear but this time Lukas seized her hand and re-directed the gear lever into the right slot.

'Once was quite enough,' he assured her. She grinned and set off through the bush at a cracking pace. Twice she saw Lukas clutch at his seat to save himself. 'You have an interesting driving style, George. You must be a favourite with London cabbies.'

'Oh, I couldn't drive in London,' she declared fervently. 'I should be scared to death. I just potter about at home sometimes.'

Lukas raised an eyebrow. 'I think it's my turn to say I don't actually believe you, Georgette. You are going out of your way to make this ride as uncomfortable as possible. If you rarely drove you would be too nervous to do that. But never mind.' She had plaited her hair in the absence of her hairpins, and he was toying with the end of her plait, twisting it around his fingers. 'Tell me what else you do when you're at home. Apart from pottering about.' There was a carelessness in his voice which didn't quite ring true.

'Nothing much,' she countered nervously, slowing down.

'Modesty doesn't quite become you, George. You've already admitted to a quantity of young relations and animals that take up all the time you're prepared to devote to photography. Do you have a job? Do you live at home

157

with your father?' He paused. 'Do you have a boyfriend?'

'I . . . share a house in London with some friends. But really, I don't drive there. It's too slow, don't you think? I have a bike.'

'What else?' He threw a glance heavenwards. 'And is one of the friends you share your house with a boyfriend?'

'Why don't you ask what you really want to know?' she said waspishly, wishing he would come to the point.

'Whatever do you mean?' he mocked her.

'Am I sleeping with one of them?' She stopped the Land Rover and turned to face him.

'I'm sure that's none of my business,' he murmured. Then, as an afterthought, 'Are you?'

'You said it, Lukas. It's really none of your business.'

'And if I wanted to make it just that?'

She took a deep breath, wanting him to make it his immediate and urgent business, but it wouldn't do. 'Don't be silly, Lukas. If you want a flirtation to pass the time you have three of the most beautiful girls I've ever seen within arm's reach.'

Lukas drew one side of his mouth down in a deprecating little smile. 'Perhaps, my dear George, but you are already installed in my tent,' he said with perfect truth.

'In that case I'll sleep in the Land Rover.'

'On your own? In the dark?'

'You're impossible! If I had thought you would take advantage of this situation — '

'I didn't invite you in, George. You gate-crashed, remember?'

'I wasn't given any choice. If I had known . . . ' She hesitated. If she had known she wouldn't have changed anything. That was the truth.

'Yes?'

'Nothing.'

'Oh, come on, Georgette. Say what you mean. What would you have done? Gone home?' He shook his head. 'I

159

don't think so. There's something that's keeping you here, making you put up with everything I'm throwing at you.' He waited for her to reply. Furiously she reached for the ignition. It had just been another ploy to get rid of her.

'This is an entirely silly conversation.'

'Why? Are you too high-principled to indulge in a mild flirtation? Does everything have to be deadly earnest?'

The engine turned but refused to catch. Furiously George tried again. 'Mild flirtation? I don't happen to think that hopping into bed with someone constitutes a mild flirtation! This is the nineties, Lukas. The century is catching up with us; didn't you know? Life *is* deadly earnest. High principles are back in fashion.'

'You're flooding the engine.'

Furiously she turned on him. 'No, I'm not!' But she stopped turning the engine over and the silence was broken only by the stridulation of the insects in the undergrowth. 'Well,' George finally demanded, 'what do we do now? Walk?'

# 6

'What a very impetuous young woman you are, Georgette. Have you no thought for your safety? You're in the middle of the bush. There could be anything out there, waiting to eat you up for lunch.'

George looked nervously around, but there was nothing out there to raise her pulse-rate the way Lukas did.

'So? What do you suggest we do?'

'I'm sure we could think of some way to pass the time.' He moved closer to her on the seat. 'Before we try the engine again.'

'Let's change places.' She moved rapidly to open the door, anxious to get out of his reach. But Lukas snapped out a hand and caught her arm.

'Certainly not.' He leaned across her and closed the door. 'Unless, of course, you're prepared to concede that you

161

need a man to get you out of trouble?'

'That's ridiculous!'

He laughed. 'I thought not. So, entertain me. Keep my mind off the terrible danger you've got us into.'

'I am not a music-hall turn, Mr Lukas,' she said coldly and, her hand shaking, she gave the key a desperate turn. After a heart-stopping effort it fired. George slipped into gear and without another word moved off, this time taking it more gently.

After a while she gave him a sideways glance from under her lashes. 'What excitement have you planned for this afternoon?' she asked.

Lukas regarded her with steady amusement for a moment and George held her breath, but he had apparently abandoned the attempt at a flirtation and returned to the business at hand, explaining the shot he had arranged earlier. He glanced at his watch. 'Come on, George, get a move on, do.'

George put her foot down, but Lukas was apparently untroubled by the shaking, hanging on without any show of discomfort. He was out of the Land Rover and walking almost before she had applied the brakes, shouting orders, making everyone jump.

'Thought we might have had a bite of lunch before starting again,' Walter muttered to George, as he heaved himself out of his camp chair.

But no one had lunch until a difficult shot of Peach taking a bush shower was successfully completed. Lukas wanted one of the little black-faced vervet monkeys to be in the shot, peeping out of a tree at her. Bait to entice it to the right spot had been laid, but the monkey was, on the whole, quicker than the camera lens.

'We could tie a piece of apple to some cotton,' George suggested after a half a dozen attempts. 'That might hold him.'

Lukas shrugged. 'The greedy little beast might fall for it.' The monkey watched suspiciously as the bait was laid once more. This time he was more cautious, but in the end he couldn't resist the temptation. He flew down the tree, made a grab for the apple and froze in astonishment as it was jerked out of reach. Then he turned and fled, gibbering at them in rage from the safety of a high branch. But it had been long enough.

For the first time since their return to camp Lukas smiled. 'Good work, team. Now, how about some lunch? I'm starving.'

By the time she had cleared away everyone had already helped themselves to lunch from the buffet and settled around the table to eat. George put some food on a plate and went to join them. By common consent the seat next to Lukas had been left vacant for her. He looked up as she sat down and smiled.

'All packed up?' She nodded. 'Excellent. We'll get off as soon as we've finished lunch.'

'Off?'

'To Nairobi. I've decided to take the

shot of Kelly with the deer this afternoon.'

George raised an eyebrow. 'How do you plan to do that? Lasso one?' Kelly, next to her, giggled. Lukas, on the other hand, allowed only the faintest quiver of his bottom lip to betray amusement.

'What a pity I hadn't thought of that. I would have enjoyed watching your attempts to round one up for us.'

'So?' she snapped. She was feeling scratchy, at odds with herself, and she knew it. Repression was, she decided, bad for you. She made an effort to pull herself together. 'Where do we get the deer from?' she asked, rather more pleasantly.

Lukas smiled appreciatively and she had the uncomfortable feeling that he knew exactly what was going on inside her head. 'There's an animal orphanage at the Nairobi National Park. It's been arranged with them — '

'Can we all come?' Peach interrupted.

'Not this time, sweetheart. There's not enough room in the plane.'

'Just make sure you take the film into Nairobi. There should be some to pick up as well.' Walter told him.

'Yes, boss,' Lukas grinned.

'And bring the newspapers.'

'And the post.'

Half an hour later they were taking off from a dirt strip alongside a game lodge just inside the nearby National Park. George used the time to write a quick note to her father to tell him that she was surviving, and to the most permanent of her 'house guests', Bob Turner, reminding him that he was to get in touch with Miss Bishop at her father's office if he was desperate for anything. She addressed the envelopes and sat back to enjoy the scenery.

'I'll put those with the rest of the post, shall I?' Lukas offered.

'They're not stamped.'

'I'll see to it.' Somewhat reluctantly she handed them over and he looked at the addresses. 'One to Daddy.' He looked up. 'And one to the boyfriend?'

'Bob's a friend, certainly. Man, rather than boy.' She was disturbed to find that she felt a definite satisfaction as Lukas's face darkened perceptibly at this information. And amusement. She didn't think that any image Lukas had of Bob was likely to coincide with the original. At sixty-two, he sported long hair — from those parts of his head that still had hair — wore a weird assortment of sixties velvet, being particularly addicted to flared trousers, and had a pierced ear from which hung a large piratical hoop.

Lukas dropped the letters into his pocket. 'We're almost there,' he said.

George looked down in fascination as the pilot banked the light aircraft over the game park. 'Look, there are some giraffes.' Almost before she could take it in they were down and rushing along the dirt runway. The five of them crammed into a waiting car and were driven to the nearby orphanage where they were met by the director.

'Everything's ready. We've screened off the far paddock to give you a bit of privacy. Bambi's already there. You can use this office for changing, make-up, or whatever. That door'll take you into the paddock.'

'Thanks.' Lukas glanced around. 'Well, we'll get on.'

The orphanage director tore his eyes from Kelly. 'Oh, right. There's a box of titbits for Bambi. If the young lady holds something in her hand Bambi will follow her anywhere.'

And she did. Kelly walked across the paddock, a thin white sarong tied carelessly across one shoulder, a shallow basket with the essential spare parts balanced on her head by one graceful hand, Bambi following to heel, and the Ngong Hills as a backdrop. Lukas was clearly pleased with the result. He glanced at his watch.

'What we need now is transport.' The director was happy to oblige. The donation to his funds for the use of his

paddock and deer had been generous.
George's eyes narrowed as she saw how
generous.

'Rather more than you paid the
villagers for their help,' she said as they
climbed into a somewhat battered
Peugeot.

'It was what they asked for, and I was
hardly in a position to say I'd go
elsewhere. It's a good cause. I thought
you supported good causes.'

'I do,' George retorted. 'I just happen
to think people are more important
than animals.'

Lukas grinned. 'Really? I thought you
would have known better. The popula-
tion of some of our animal species is
already at crisis point. I hadn't noticed
that problem with people.'

George glared. 'You know what I
mean.'

'Of course I do.' He reached across
and patted her hand patronisingly.
'Now, what are we all going to do in
Nairobi?'

'You can drop me at the Norfolk,'

Kelly replied. 'I want to phone John and have a bath.' Mark and Suzy had similar plans.

'That's it, then.' He pulled up outside the hotel. 'You can take the post and the films. Make sure you pick up everything. I'll collect you later.' George made a move to follow them, but Lukas stopped her. 'Don't go.'

She looked at him blankly. 'I could do with a bath as well.'

'If that was an invitation I could be persuaded to change my mind.' His face was deadly serious. 'And I'd scrub your back,' he offered hopefully. George twitched away from his gaze, well aware that bright spots of colour were burning her cheeks. 'No? Pity. In that case I insist you help me with an errand of mercy instead.'

George was immediately remorseful. 'Michael! You're going to visit him.'

'You'd forgotten! I find it hard to believe that someone with your heightened sense of patronage would have forgotten a person in need.'

She shook off his hand and slammed the car door. 'We'd better get some grapes.'

'The fruit market is just down the road.' Grinning happily at her discomfort, he pulled up outside the market and found a coin for the parking meter. 'Come along, sourpuss. It's no good sulking just because you're not the only one with good intentions.'

'That's unfair!'

'Well, smile, then. Take off those silly glasses, and enjoy yourself. Then I'll try to stop teasing you.' George suddenly felt foolish. She was being shrewish. Had been ever since Lukas had hinted at a mild flirtation. And she knew why. Slowly she reached up and removed the tinted glasses. She folded them and slipped them into her bag.

'Is that better?' Her voice was husky. She cleared her throat. 'Is . . . ?'

'Much better.' Lukas plucked her hat from her head and dropped it in a nearby bin.

'Hey!'

He ignored her protest; instead he removed the band fastening her plait and ran his fingers through her hair to loosen it, shaking it free before capturing her face in his hands.

'Lukas! Let me go!' she demanded, only too conscious that several people had slowed down to watch, enjoying the unexpected sideshow.

He smiled, then bent to place a kiss firmly on her mouth. 'There,' he said, with satisfaction. 'That's much better.' He released her before she could protest.

'Why did you do that?' she demanded.

'It was you or the hat. Frankly, I prefer you.'

'That's not what . . . ' She stopped.

'Yes?' He was laughing at her. Shakily she tugged her fingers through her hair. 'I must look a mess,' she said lamely.

'You look quite beautiful.' He gazed at her for a moment. 'I should be surprised, but somehow I'm not. Now. Grapes.' He took her hand and led her across the road and up the steps into the market where George came abruptly to a halt.

'What flowers!' she exclaimed, stunned by the exotics mixed with the humbler carnations. 'And the scent! I didn't think tropical flowers had a scent.'

The stallholder held out the white blooms. Lukas nodded and indicated some roses. 'Red?' he asked her.

'They won't last.'

Lukas raised a mocking brow. 'What does? Enjoy them while they do.'

She bit her lip, feeling foolish. Lukas was clearly a practised flirt. 'Perhaps it would be better if . . . '

'Yes?' he prompted, holding out a bunch of grapes for her inspection. She nodded.

It was too ridiculous. It was nothing but a game for him. 'Nothing. Why don't you get him some tangerines as well?'

'Good idea.'

★ ★ ★

Michael was propped up, his leg covered by a cage. The table across his bed was covered in small glass jars full of the specimens he had collected and he was busy writing when they arrived.

'Lukas! Good of you to come.' He eyed George with interest.

'We finished early at the orphanage, so we thought we had better come and bring you some grapes.'

'Bless you. The grapes are most welcome. But so is the vision of loveliness you have brought with you.'

'You've been in here too long, Michael,' Lukas tutted. 'This is George. She is not a vision of anything. She is an assistant.'

Michael looked over his spectacles at George and then at Lukas. He laughed. 'Yes, well. Anyone can see that. But I don't recall ever rating a bunch of red roses.' His gaze returned to George. 'You're my replacement, I take it?'

'Georgette Bainbridge. How do you do?'

He took her proffered hand. 'Why

don't you sit down?'

'We're interrupting your work.' George glanced at the specimen collection and looked quickly away again. 'I'm surprised they allow you to have those in here.'

'Oh, they're all right. They're dead.' He looked at Lukas. 'They wouldn't let me have Dido.'

'Dido?' George looked from one to the other.

'I'd forgotten Dido.' Lukas smiled thoughtfully. 'She is a quite delightful little hunting spider that Mike found in the mess tent.'

'Oh, come on, Lukas. She isn't little. She's a fine specimen. They're looking after her for me at the snake farm. You could go and see her if you like.'

'No.' George was rooted to the spot. She took several deep breaths while the two men watched her with amusement.

The bottles, with their leggy contents, seemed to be coming nearer and nearer. George felt an urgent desire to run. Only Lukas and his laughing mouth kept her glued to the spot. He placed an arm around her shoulders and unconsciously she moved closer to him. Michael noticed the movement with a twitch of his lips.

'Well, I'd better let you young things run along and enjoy yourselves. Think of me, stuck in bed, with nothing but the odd dead spider to keep me company. I say, Lukas. You could bring Dido to visit. I'm sure they'd allow that.'

'Forget it. I'll see you soon.'

George lifted her hand a few inches. 'Bye.'

Lukas led her stiffly to the car park and sat her in the car. 'I thought you weren't afraid of spiders,' he grinned.

George swallowed. 'I'm not. In theory. In practice, I might just be a little bit . . . terrified.'

'Come on. I'll buy you a drink.' He started the car. 'Unless you'd rather go on and meet Dido?'

'The drink will do just fine,' George said firmly. 'Thank you.'

'We'll go to the club for a sundowner. I think we're just about respectable enough to eat on the terrace there.'

They sat on the terrace of the Nairobi Club, sipping their icy drinks and regarding one another silently. George examined the planes and angles of her companion's face in the rapidly fading light with undisguised interest. At last Lukas grinned. 'Well?'

'It's an interesting face. I should like to take a portrait. If I may?'

'Only if you promise to hang it beside that of the Princess Royal. What else?'

She put her head to one side and narrowed her eyes. 'It's not a British face. The cheekbones are too wide. You're too dark.'

'Does that matter?' he asked, a sudden watchfulness shadowing his eyes.

'No.' She thought for a moment. 'Thirtyish. Thirty-three or thirty-four?'

'Thirty-two. I've had a hard life.'

'Have you?' She picked up his hand, lying on the table between them. It was strong and tanned and sprinkled lightly with dark hair. She turned it over. The fingers were long and tapering, the palms free of calluses. 'Not manual labour. In what way hard?' She looked up and too late saw the dangerous glint of laughter, and the teasing curve of his mouth. She dropped the hand as if stung, but he caught her fingers and pulled her hand across the table towards him. 'Let go!' she demanded.

'It's my turn,' he said with a hurt expression. He sat forward and gazed into her eyes, her fingers clasped between his. 'An interesting face. I should like to take a portrait, if I may?' he asked with the utmost seriousness.

'Perhaps.' She was discouraging.

'A very English face. Peachy skin. Dark blue — no, violet eyes. And that high, almost medieval forehead.' His thick dark brows drew together slightly and he paused, his face suddenly intent. 'Very much in the style of a Raphael madonna.' He carried on, but she had the feeling that it was formality; the fun had suddenly gone out of it. 'Young. Twentyish?' he suggested.

'Twenty-two.'

'That old?' He feigned surprise.

'I've had an easy life,' she replied in an effort to keep it a game.

He lifted her hand to examine it, and before she could retract it had dropped a kiss into the palm. 'Certainly not a lot of bricklaying.'

The appearance of smoked salmon enabled George to reclaim her hand and attempt to still the fluttering in her abdomen. Twice George caught Lukas staring at her with a disquieting expression as he ate his food. The waiter cleared their plates and they sat in silence, waiting for their cutlets. The atmosphere between them was no longer light. A dangerous undertow was tugging George out of her depth.

They both started to speak at once, and stopped. 'Please. You first,' Lukas invited politely.

Still George hesitated. Perhaps she had just imagined the recognition in the

179

unwavering grey eyes. But Lukas was waiting and she plunged in, suddenly unable to bear the tension a moment longer. 'You've remembered, haven't you?' She faltered before the intensity of his gaze.

'I knew the day you arrived that we had met before. But I have to admit your disguise was good. Every time I started to think about it you did something tiresome enough to distract me. It was very clever, Georgette.'

'So. What made you finally remember?'

'As soon as I heard myself describing your forehead as medieval. That was what struck me on the last occasion we met.' He allowed a smile to widen his mouth. 'Prior to the bag of flour.' She had expected him to be angry, but instead he seemed rather to be amused by her predicament. 'I was fascinated by your face. I wasn't in the least bit interested in those poor girls parading for my attention. I had an image of you hammering in my head. It was so clear that all I could think of was asking you to sit for me. To get you out of those clothes and — '

She didn't want to hear what he had planned. 'Did you get your jacket back?' she interrupted him sharply. The waiter placed a plate in front of her and began to serve.

His eyes flickered in surprise at her abrupt intervention. 'Yes. I got it back. Thank you for having it cleaned. Rather an odd gesture, I thought, in the circumstances.'

She retreated to politeness. 'It was the least I could do. It wasn't meant to be personal.' But it had been — once he had begun to devour her with those unsmiling slate eyes. Once she had realised that she wanted to be devoured.

'It felt very personal. And I can assure you that my response was entirely personal. I'd do it again.' A sudden sparkle lit the back of his eyes. 'With the utmost pleasure.'

She swallowed. 'What will you do

now? Send me home?'

He looked at her with curiosity. 'It's important to you, isn't it? Staying here?' She nodded dumbly. He sat back and regarded her thoughtfully. 'I was sorry I let you go so easily the last time we met. In fact I tried to find you, but no one seemed to know who you were.'

'You should have left me to be arrested,' she said with some feeling. 'Then my name would have been in the papers.'

'Perhaps. But it was more fun my way, wouldn't you say? I'll make you a proposition, Georgette. We have unfinished business, you and I. If I let you stay, will you sit for me?'

George felt the heat colouring her face. He wanted her to pose for him. She swallowed. 'Here?' she asked, her voice hardly above a whisper.

He shook his head. 'No. In my studio.' His smile was not reassuring. 'It's more private.'

There was a tight band fastening about her chest, making it difficult for her to breathe. 'I could change my mind once we leave Kenya.'

'I don't believe you would go back on a promise given, Georgette.' There was a soft conviction in his voice.

'No.'

'Think about it.' He picked up his knife and fork and attacked his food with sudden enthusiasm. When he looked up again, there was no trace of threat in his face, only a friendly smile. 'You can tell me when we pick up the others. If you decide to go home I'll leave you at the Norfolk.'

George played with her food, trying to decide if it would matter. The mere taking off of her clothes was nothing. If it had been anybody else it would be nothing. But the thought of revealing herself for Lukas was turning her slowly to jelly.

He made no comment on her untouched food, instead he glanced at his watch. 'We'd better pick the others up.' He signed the bill and began to rise.

'Lukas!' The urgency in her voice stopped him. 'Who would see the photograph? Would you use it for . . . a calendar?'

His face betrayed no emotion. 'Is that all you see when you look at me, Georgette?' He shook his head. 'You're so damned narrow-minded. Don't you have a use for the wretched things? Haven't you ever had one with reproductions of famous paintings, for instance? Botticelli's *Birth of Venus*? The *Naked Maja*?' She looked at her hands, anywhere, but at him. 'For your information the MotorPart calendar is the only one I do. It's a special favour for your father, and I make sure he pays for the privilege. The money buys me time for other things.' He saw the mute appeal in her eyes and relented. 'No one but me will see the portrait I take of you.' He drew her to her feet. 'No one else will be at the studio. It will be just for me. And I too keep my word.'

He tucked her arm into his and led her back to the car. As he opened the passenger door for her the scent of the flowers rose up to fill the night air. It was overwhelming, suffocating almost. Lukas picked up the posy and handed it to her. 'They were a mistake, I think. Madonna lilies would suit you better. I must remember that.'

She took the flowers and he helped her into the car.

'You're trembling, George,' he drawled softly.

'I'm feeling a bit chilly,' she countered.

'I could warm you up,' he offered with a gentleness she chose to ignore.

'No doubt.'

He shrugged and did not speak again until they pulled up in front of the Norfolk.

George barely noticed the others crowding into the rear of the car. An unspoken question lay between them and Lukas was waiting for an answer. His arm was draped casually across the back of the seat, but there was a tension about his eyes as he waited for her decision.

'George?'

She tore her eyes away from the intensity of his gaze and glanced towards the hotel, knowing that she should walk away from him while she still could.

'Hadn't we better be going, Lukas?'

# 7

There was the faintest glint of satisfaction about his eyes as Lukas regarded her from his seat beside the pilot. George regretted the impulse that had driven her to scramble into the back of the plane to be as far from him as possible. She had no wish to be separated from him by even a few feet — it left her too much time to consider the consequences of what she had promised.

It seemed an odd chain of events that had led her from a demonstration against a beauty competition to the point at which she had agreed to pose for Lukas. She stared at the back of his head where unruly dark hair curled over the back of his collar, and wondered what it would be like, what he would ask her to do. The small sound that escaped her throat was nothing to do with the pilot's warning that they were about to land.

They hit the deck with a bump and the plane raced towards a distant light. When they finally taxied to a halt George saw with a shock that it was nothing but a pair of car headlights. The pilot helped them unload their equipment. George and Lukas both reached for the tripod at the same time and their hands touched. George withdrew as if she'd been stung.

He looked up, surprised by her reaction. 'I don't bite,' he murmured softly. She didn't, couldn't answer as he shouldered it and stowed it alongside the camera and film boxes.

He opened the passenger door for her and she clambered up quickly, squeezing against the jeep to avoid the dangerous pleasure of touching him.

For a moment he swayed towards her, oblivious to their interested audience. 'Regretting your decision already, George?' he asked, quiet anger in every syllable. 'Well, it's too late to change your mind now.' He shut the door firmly.

George felt her fingernails bite into the palm of her hands. Her problem was not regret, but that she couldn't keep the idea of it out of her head.

The drive through the bush was a dark nightmare. Lukas drove with a wild recklessness, forcing her to hang on as they hurtled along the rough track. The eruption of a nightjar, into the glare of the headlights, brought a small cry from George.

'For God's sake, it was only a bird!'

'I'm sorry,' George apologised in a small voice, but he completed the journey at a steadier rate, without a further break in the tense silence. Their arrival was greeted with an almost uniform sigh of relief and for a moment everyone sat completely still. Then Walter's face appeared at George's window.

'Did the transparencies arrive?'

Work brought them all back to life and minutes later they were bent in concentration over the portable light box. 'They're pretty good,' Lukas finally remarked. 'That worked really well.' George looked at the slides, but they had all been taken before she arrived and her opinion was apparently unsought. She turned to go. Without turning from his contemplation of the photographs Lukas put out a hand and captured her wrist, pulling her back. He let go just long enough to put his arm around her waist and draw her close against him. He looked down, his eyes cold granite chips only inches from her own.

'What do you think of this one, George?' he drawled. The question, the tone, was amiable. Only she could see his eyes and understood the implicit challenge. This, he was saying, this is what you will do for me. She felt the colour drain from her face.

'I think it's . . . ' she struggled for a suitable adjective ' . . . very nice.' He wasn't the only one who could say one thing and mean something entirely different. She pulled free from his restraining arm. 'I think I'll go to bed, if you'll excuse me.' And, with a calmness that surprised her, she turned and walked away.

'Do you think you can manage by yourself tonight?' His voice carried across the camp, bringing her to a halt. 'If not, will you leave your pyjamas out? I had the devil's own job finding them last night.'

She stumbled as her knees sagged. Before she could recover herself Lukas was there, holding her arm, supporting her.

'I'm sorry. George, please forgive me. I shouldn't have done that.' She was too shaken to register that concern, and something warmer, had replaced the cold anger in his eyes.

'Did you? Put me to bed?' But she didn't need to ask. It was quite obvious he had. She recalled his amusement when she had said she couldn't remember going to bed. The last thing she remembered was lying down and

191

then it was morning.

'Come on, my love. I'll light the lamp for you.' He led her stiff body to the tent but she could not, would not go inside.

'George?' But she stood with her toes digging into the ground through her shoes, refusing to budge. He responded by putting an arm around her waist and picking her up. He held her against his chest and she could feel his heart beating fast as he kept her close.

'No!' she whispered desperately, but he took no notice. He smiled suddenly and ducked inside.

'Put me down,' she pleaded with him.

'Will you forgive me?' he insisted.

'Forgive you?' she demanded. 'How can I? I don't know what you did.' Desperately she tried to shake free of him, but he wouldn't release her and she knew that if she didn't make him let her go it would be too late for both of them. She tried again. 'Did you enjoy yourself? Undo the buttons one by one?

Have a good look?' He didn't answer. 'Well?'

He merely smiled. 'I meant forgive me for shouting it to the world, Georgette. I didn't do anything to you that I need be ashamed of.'

His calmness incensed her. 'Well, that's really reassuring. I'm supposed to believe that — '

His mouth cut off the words and his kiss destroyed the last shreds of resistance she had clung to.

Lukas groaned and at last set her on her feet, holding her against him, staring at her as if he had never seen her before. 'Damn you, Georgette Bainbridge. What is it about you that stops me behaving rationally?' His lips fluttered over her eyes. 'Two days and I've been bewitched.' He looked down at her and shook his head. 'I'm too old to feel like this.'

'I'm not,' George breathed.

From the moment his mouth took possession of her, she acknowledged that it had been inevitable, the sparring between them nothing but mental foreplay. She had been waiting for this, wanting it ever since he had crossed the lobby of the Norfolk Hotel and turned his disbelieving eyes upon her. Now her senses were swimming with pleasure and she moaned in protest when he lifted his head to stare at her in amazement.

'Dear God! This can't be real.'

'Lukas . . . ' She reached up and laced her fingers in his dark wayward hair. But she didn't need to beg. Already his lips had reclaimed hers, firing her with a desperate need as desire flickered and ignited under his expert touch. He shifted his grip, seeking the buttons that fastened her shirt and flicking them effortlessly apart. George arched towards him as long fingers brushed aside the lace cup of her bra, seeking a nipple already hard and aching for his touch. Nothing had ever prepared her for this onslaught upon her senses and she was totally without defences . . . ready to submit to a man she barely knew . . . more than ready . . .

'Lukas!' Walter's voice was sharp outside the tent.

'What the hell . . . ?' And he groaned as he straightened and stared down at her. 'I'll be right with you, Walter.'

'No!' Her voice came out a long, low, hungering moan as he released her and fumbled for the matches. At the second attempt he managed to light the gas lamp. 'Don't leave me, Lukas,' she begged.

He gripped the table hard and she could see his knuckles whiten in the gaslight. His face was ashen as he turned to George. 'I think it would be better if you were asleep when I come back,' he said thickly before disappearing through the opening.

'Lukas, I warned you . . . '

'I just had a bit of trouble with the lamp, Walter. Now, what are we going to do tomorrow . . . ?' His voice faded as they walked back to the mess tent.

George sank on to her camp bed,

weak with frustrated longing. She curled up and hugged herself, pressing her legs together tightly to deny the urgent need Lukas had awoken in her, calling him every name she could think of for abandoning her in such a state.

For a while she was sure he must come back. Had to come back to her. But he didn't come and all that was left to do was go to bed, by herself. She pulled back the sheet. A small spider, startled by the sudden light, flattened itself in panic against the bed. George stared at it for a moment and then with an impatient gesture she scooped it up and threw it out into the night.

She knew she wouldn't sleep. She didn't even bother to try. Instead she picked up the book she had brought with her: *Memoirs of a Dutiful Daughter*. She had read it a long time ago, and had bought the paperback copy at the airport, amused by the aptness of the title. It would no doubt repay a second look.

There was no sound from Lukas as she poured herself a cup of tea in the hooded light of the torch, and she took it through to the wash tent where she dressed in her favourite designer jeans, firmly tucking in a white T-shirt to reveal the generous line of her figure and her narrow waist. There was no further point in playing the dowd, she thought, as she vigorously brushed her hair and left it to hang loose in a shining curtain around her shoulders.

Satisfied with the result, she made her bed. Lukas groaned and turned over. 'Must you make so much noise?' he demanded, and then subsided, clearly wishing he hadn't spoken.

'Would you like a cup of tea?' George asked, examining with serenity his forlorn expression. He had stumbled in at some unearthly hour and fallen on to the camp bed. She had pretended to be asleep and for a while she had resolutely rejected the attractive notion of undressing him.

'You haven't, by any chance, got something for a bad head, have you?'

Expressionless, she produced a packet of painkillers from her bag and poured a glass of water from the flask on the table. 'These might help,' she said, without sympathy. He had, after all, no one but himself to blame. If he had stayed and made love to her he wouldn't be in such a miserable condition.

'I doubt it,' he growled but took them and swallowed the water, then lay back with a groan. George poured him a cup of tea and left him to it.

She sat alongside the river, waiting for the dawn, and allowed herself a forlorn smile. It had been too good an opportunity to miss. Too perfect a revenge for his public humiliation of her, for his abandonment . . .

She had lain in the darkness until even breathing announced that he was dead to the world. Her eyes, already accustomed to the darkness by her long, wakeful vigil, had had no trouble in finding the buttons of his blue denim shirt. He had obviously started to undo them, but given up the effort. She had rapidly finished the job and eased the shirt up his back and over his head, trying not to think about his warm skin pressed against the thin silk of her pyjamas, and the well-built athletic body she had seen in all its splendour only that morning.

She had examined his sleeping face. He had a rugged sort of beauty in repose, and she had gently traced the outline of his jaw with her fingers. She had thought of him as someone she barely knew, but that wasn't true. He had been a part of her since their first meeting. His kiss had woken a sleeping passion in her that she had chosen to believe was anger, and perhaps that had been a part of it. But you couldn't stay angry with someone for three years without them carving a deep impression into your heart.

She had kissed him lightly on the mouth and wondered if he had taken the same liberty. She hoped he had. She had slipped the button of his trousers and pulled down the zip, easing them over his narrow hips and down dangerously long legs. A pair of very large bush boots had prevented their removal and she pulled them off. George had stood up and surveyed her victim, lying full length, defenceless in only a pair of white boxer shorts. She had hesitated, sensing a change in his breathing. With the faintest smile she had pulled a sheet over him.

'Coward,' he'd murmured, and she had flown back to the relative safety of her own bed, her cheeks burning.

Around her the birds began to shift and fidget now, and from the tent she heard a crash and a muffled curse. She packed away her camera and her fingers only shook a little as she dismantled the tripod.

She was sitting at the breakfast table making notes when Lukas appeared. His challenging expression, daring her to gloat, momentarily dented her composure. Then he sank into a chair and ran a hand over his unshaven face and she longed to comfort him, make him feel better. She firmly quashed the notion.

'Coffee?' she asked. He didn't answer, but she poured him a cup and placed it in front of him. He made a noise that might have been 'thanks', but she couldn't be sure. 'Can I get you some fruit?' He glared at her, then winced, as if even the movement of his face was too much to bear. She piled some grapefruit into a dish and placed it in front of him. 'Vitamin C is recommended for a hangover, I believe.'

'And what's recommended for a surfeit of self-control?'

'Self-control?' Her voice shook slightly.

'Wouldn't you say I was excessively self-controlled when you practically raped me last night?' He glowered and then, clearly wishing he hadn't, rubbed his eyes. 'Let me tell you, madam, that I am rather more the gentleman than you are a lady.'

'I think that's a pity,' she said, and

then felt the colour surge hotly to her cheeks.

'Come on, George. It won't do. You've been forced to share a tent with me. I can't possibly take advantage of the situation.'

'That's what Walter said, is it?' She saw from his expression that she had got it right.

She retired behind her newspaper until the steward brought her a plateful of sausage, bacon and fried aubergine. She stared at it for a moment, wondering how on earth she had thought she could eat it. Then she smiled at the steward.

'Thank you. It looks wonderful. Could you pass the salt, please, Lukas?' He looked up from the gloomy contemplation of his coffee and caught sight of her food and groaned. He stood up suddenly, his chair going over with a crash, and disappeared, clutching his mouth.

George looked at the steward. 'I don't think Mr. Lukas will want any breakfast this morning, Kubwa. But you'd better bring some more coffee.'

The others gradually drifted in and helped themselves to breakfast, Kelly sitting so long in dreamy-eyed contemplation of a slice of pineapple that George asked if anything was the matter.

'She's mooning over her boyfriend,' Peach sneered. 'He writes for the gossip page of the *Chronicle*.'

George appeared suitably impressed and, encouraged, Kelly went on. 'I was telling him all about poor Michael's accident and you having to come and take his place. He was ever so interested. He asked if you were Sir Charles Bainbridge's daughter, and I said yes. I was right, wasn't I?'

George nodded wordlessly, a sinking feeling in the pit of her stomach. 'Yes, you were quite right.' She didn't bother to ask what interesting little details he had managed to extract from the guileless Kelly. She thought that on the whole she would rather not know.

When Lukas reappeared his colour had returned somewhat, but his temper had not. He snapped, without prejudice, at everyone who came under his eye. It was just George's hard luck that she was closest for most of the time, and came in for more than her fair share of bile. That she refused to be intimidated seemed only to make him worse.

Peach had the misfortune to be the subject for the first session. She suffered half an hour of the sort of remarks that would have turned most men to jelly, but it took the suggestion that she had a blemish on her chin to finally reduce her to a flood of tears. Walter bore down on Lukas with an expression that sent George scurrying to cut him off. 'Go and sort out Peach,' she encouraged and, taking a can of drink, went after Lukas. She found him sitting on a fallen tree. He looked up as she approached and his mouth tightened.

'Go away, George. I want to be on

my own.' Ignoring his words, she sat down beside him. She opened the can and handed it to him.

'How's your head?' she asked.

'Foul.'

She grinned. 'There's some justice, then.'

'Bitch,' he replied, but without emphasis. 'What do you want from me, George?'

For a moment she was tempted to tell him exactly what she wanted, but this wasn't the time, or the place.

'I want you to act like a professional, Lukas. It's what you expect from the rest of us. There was absolutely no need for you to get drunk last night. But you did, and you must pay for it. You've made us all suffer for quite long enough.'

She stood up and started back the way she had come. He caught her arm before she had gone ten yards. She looked pointedly at his hand. 'Please let go of me.'

His eyes silently challenged her to

make him and she met him head-on. He inclined his head slightly and finally released her and ran his hand distractedly through thick dark curls. 'George, this is ridiculous. What are we going to do?'

'Do?' She remained completely still for a moment, trying to dismiss from her mind the memory of his mouth on hers, his caressing touch. 'You are the best judge of that, but I imagine the most sensible thing would be to get this shot taken and get back to camp.'

\* \* \*

'You're not coming to the races with us?' Walter enquired with surprise, over breakfast one morning.

Lukas stared pointedly at George. 'I have been volunteered for a bricklaying party.' He glanced around the table. 'You can all come. The more the merrier.'

There were no recruits for this unattractive proposition but Walter was interested. 'Bricklaying doesn't seem quite your scene, dear boy. I thought you enjoyed the turf.'

'On this occasion I shall have to miss it. Just make sure you bring me back a motorbike. I want to take that last shot tomorrow.'

'I'll do my best.'

'I'm not interested in your best. Just do it. And take Michael the Sunday papers. They should arrive before lunch.'

'Have a good time, all of you,' George told them and handed some money to Kelly. 'Put this on something with a pretty name for me.'

'Each way or to win?'

'To win,' she said recklessly, then retreated to the tent before Lukas could comment.

They had done their best to avoid being alone together since the evening they went to Nairobi. He no longer slept in the tent but she was sure that she was the only person who knew that. Instead he took himself off to the Land Rover at night and she rose long before dawn so that he could come and wash. It was an arrangement arrived at by unspoken agreement.

She had assumed that he would choose to forget about taking her to the school building party and go to the races with the others. Instead, she was going to be left on her own with him, so the sooner she was ready to leave the better.

She had gathered her belongings when she heard the jeep roar out of the camp. She checked she had everything and turned to go. Lukas was standing in the opening, watching her. Despite the oldest clothes he had been able to find — a pair of torn jeans and a black T-shirt from which the sleeves had been ripped, probably years before — he looked unbearably desirable.

George was keeping a tight hold on her emotions, not allowing a tremor of what she felt to show. But it was hard.

'They've gone. We're on our own.' There was nothing particularly threatening in this statement, but nevertheless

George felt a quiver of apprehension.

'Yes. Well, it's time for us to be off too.'

'You'll need a hat.' He was twisting a baseball cap in his hands with the MotorPart logo emblazoned on the front. She regarded it with disfavour.

'I had a perfectly good hat until you binned it,' she pointed out with perfect truth.

'Wear this,' he ordered, thrusting the cap at her. 'We'll be out in the sun all day, and I haven't the time or the inclination to rush you into Nairobi if you get sunstroke.'

George crackled with resentment as she took it from him. 'Don't worry, Lukas. I'd lie in the bush and die before I asked you to waste your time on anything so trivial!'

He leaned over her, a frightening glint in his eyes. 'Is that so?' he rasped.

George stepped back quickly, intimidated by the fierce figure dominating her in the confined space, but found a tent pole at her back. 'What's the matter, Georgette? Nervous?'

She swallowed. Of course she was nervous. She had been alone for no more that a minute with this man she had fallen insanely, stupidly in love with. Already the air was crackling with sexual tension and one word from him would be enough. She would be lost.

'N-no,' she denied uselessly.

Without warning he swooped. His arm snaked around her waist and he dragged her against his hard chest.

'Foolish . . . foolish . . . ' He held her fast with his eyes as slowly, oh, so slowly, he bent over her. A small cry escaped her and she tensed as his mouth closed the space between them and she shut her eyes tight to blot out the dark brooding eyes so close to her own. Then in a sudden panic she began to fight. She beat on hard, sinewy arms without effect and he grinned, holding her without effort. Finally, inevitably, she gave up. 'That's better. Now stand still, wretched girl. I'm going to make love to you.'

She held herself rigid, expecting him to be cruel, punishing, but his kiss took her by surprise. It was gentle, teasing, infinitely more dangerous. For a long moment she managed to retain control against the insistence of his mouth, but gradually her body betrayed her, relaxing against him, languorous pleasure suffusing every limb. Her lips parted under the sensuous probing of his tongue, and she responded shamelessly, pressing against him as desire flickered and ignited under his expert touch.

He shifted his grip on her, pulling free the shirt tucked into her jeans, flicking open the buttons one by one and peeling it off her with ease. He slipped his hand inside her bra and cupped a breast aching for his touch, and bent to kiss its rosy tip. She trembled, her legs buckling beneath her, her only support his arm pinioning her, defenceless as a butterfly, against the tent pole. She arched in brazen welcome, feeling his hard desire for her, and wanting him desperately in return.

'Lukas . . . ' she gasped, and then she staggered abruptly as the tent began to sway and the pole she was leaning against tilted drunkenly. They collapsed in a heap together as the ridge pole descended, missing them by inches, and George found herself gazing up at the thunderstruck face of Lukas.

'Is that what they mean when they say the earth moved?' she asked, breathlessly.

He groaned. 'Something moved. It felt more like the sky.' He made no move to disentagle himself from her. 'Are you all right?'

'I think so.'

'Good.' He resumed where he had left off . . .

'*Bwana*? *Memsahib*? Are you there? Are you alive?'

'Damn!' Then Lukas grinned philosophically. 'The trouble with this place is that there are just too many people about.' He kissed her lightly then helped her find her shirt. She clambered awkwardly into it under the canvas, before they crawled sheepishly out of the remains of their tent. 'I'm sorry about that, my friend,' Lukas apologised. 'Can it be put back together?' George found herself irritated by his self-possession, while her emotions were all anyhow.

The steward nodded vigorously. 'Will do, will do. No trouble.'

As they walked towards the Land Rover Lukas took her hand. 'I was quite unaware that lovemaking in a tent was such a hazardous affair.'

George shook her head. 'I'm sure he thought we were going to blame him for the collapse of the tent.'

Lukas gave her an odd look. 'If that's what you want to think, George, I won't disabuse you. But anyone with an atom of sense can see what caused the tent to collapse just by looking at you.'

She blushed furiously, and stopped to tuck her shirt firmly back in place. She raked her fingers through her hair and placed the baseball cap that she was carrying on her head.

'Is that better?' she asked.

'I preferred you as you were.' Lukas opened the Land Rover door for her with a satisfied smirk that she could have slapped. 'But, since you're asking, I think your buttons could do with a little adjustment.' She looked down and saw that she had missed the top two buttons. Her fingers were shaking too much to cope with the adjustment. He pulled her shirt out and began to undo the buttons. She tried to stop him, but he kissed her and completed the job.

'I should feel as guilty as hell for taking advantage of a girl who's been forced to share a tent with me.'

'So what's changed your mind, Lukas?'

'Because, my sweet, after your fun and games the other night I have very strong doubts that I'll be the one doing the taking.'

'Despite the fact that I'm the boss's daughter?'

'Damn Walter. Has he said something to you?'

She shook her head. 'It didn't take a lot of working out.' She looked him full in the face. 'But I'm grown up, Lukas. Even my father wouldn't have presumed to interfere in the way that Walter did. I make my own decisions and I expect you to do the same.'

He digested this information, then nodded. 'I'll bear that in mind.' For a moment she thought he was going to do something about it there and then. Instead, he helped her into the Land Rover and she couldn't decide whether she was pleased or not.

At the village George and Lukas were greeted as honoured guests. She had brought a small gift of cash for the school fund and was applauded politely. Lukas had brought a case of beer which was received with considerably more enthusiasm. He immediately joined the work, stripping off his T-shirt in the heat as the effort of lifting increased in direct proportion to the height of the wall.

George watched him with discreet pleasure through the lens of her camera, using her zoom to capture a sudden laugh, his well-muscled back shiny with sweat, a powerful man enjoying hard work. He looked up and caught her once, his eyes burning her through the prying lens, and she felt suddenly, ridiculously shy.

Afterwards there was beer, and a group of young girls began to dance. George leaned against Lukas, soaking in the simple pleasure of their closeness and his arm about her waist. When she was surrounded by the dancers, wanting her to join in, she scrambled to her feet reluctantly. But two of the girls took her hands and showed her the steps, encouraging her as she caught the rhythm. The men joined in and the dance struck a more urgent, primeval note. Lukas needed no second bidding to join in the raw thrusting motion, holding her in his possession with nothing but his compelling grey eyes.

When the drumming stopped they sank to the ground with relief. George fanned herself with her discarded hat and found Lukas regarding her solemnly.

'You've no idea, have you?' he asked.

'No idea? What about?'

'I've just claimed you.' He indicated the village. 'Everyone now regards us as betrothed.' Lukas drained a can of beer as she thoughtfully regarded their dancing companions, scattered in couples, talking quietly together, just as she and Lukas were.

'You're making that up,' was the only reasonable response that came to mind, but she wished he wasn't.

Lukas pretended to look offended. 'I had to dance hard to get you. That chap over there tried to cut me out.' He considered her still flushed face. 'Perhaps you'd have preferred that? Or are you already spoken for? The 'man' friend you wrote to, perhaps?'

'Bob?' For a moment she was going to laugh, then the look in his eyes stopped her. Before she could explain, they were summoned to join in the feast but as soon as they were decently able to leave the celebrations he took her hand firmly and possessively in his.

'It's time to be going, George.'

# 8

Making no move to resist him, George allowed Lukas to lead her to the Land Rover. The sun was already setting and in the east a star sparkled against the darkening sky as they drove carefully homewards. They startled a jackal crossing the track, about his evening business, but apart from that and the singing of the cicadas they might have been alone on the planet. Lukas reached out and took hold of her hand.

The camp was in darkness when they arrived. 'Alone at last,' Lukas joked, lifting her down. He continued to hold her lightly around the waist for a moment and pulled her to him, letting her feel how much he wanted her.

'Well?' he asked softly, the question loaded with the possibilities that lay before them, but he made no move to claim her. The decision was to be hers alone. He wouldn't use his body, or her own, to pressure her. They stood together in the quiet circle of his arms while George examined her unique response. It was not the first time a man had suggested she might like to join him in bed. What was unique was the fact that she wanted to say yes. Longed to say yes.

In answer she put her arms around his neck and pulled his head down, offering her lips, letting the love she had kept in tight rein flood from her and envelop him.

'Oh, my love.' His voice was a husky murmur. Then he kissed her, his tongue gently exploring the sweetness of her mouth. When he released her his eyes were dark with passion and a deep excitement that sent a shiver through her.

'Could we . . . ?' She blushed at her own audacity. 'Could we have a shower? First?' she added, in case he should think she was trying to back out.

He dropped the lightest kiss on her

forehead and smiled. 'I do realise that I'm not very savoury.' He laughed at her embarrassment. 'I have been working rather hard. But since you're offering . . . ' he was suddenly serious ' . . . I can't imagine anything I would enjoy more than a shower with you. First.' He swept up their belongings from the back seat of the Land Rover and carried them across to their tent, his other arm looped around her waist. 'Hold on, I'll light a lamp.'

He dropped the things he was carrying on his bed and struck a match. As the lamp flared George saw, lying among the things Lukas had carried from the Land Rover, a slightly battered newspaper. Even as she moved to retrieve it, he gathered it up with her camera.

'I'll pick up another lamp for the shower.' He glanced down to see what she was staring at. 'Did you want this? It's days old,' he remarked without interest and just for a moment she thought she was safe. Then he saw the photograph. A sudden stillness about him sent her heart crashing to her boots. His face when he looked up at her had lost all gentleness.

'So, sweet Georgette, everything becomes clear. Now I can see why you were sent here. Despite the fact that you clearly didn't want to come. Didn't even know what you had come to do. Tell me, do you keep a diary? Will you earn extra Brownie points for managing to soothe the savage Lukas in full hangover?' He glared at her. 'Well, watch me. You might just have to do that all over again. Because that's what all this is about, isn't it? Getting back in Daddy's good books. What did he do, George? Cut you off without a penny and put you on punishment duty?'

'Pa — ' She would have told him. Explained about the refuge and what it meant to her, but he didn't give her the chance.

'So much for all your much vaunted high ideals,' he goaded her. 'What did you do? Put them on hold until you're forgiven? Until the parental purse is restored?' He ignored the dangerous patches of red staining her cheeks. He took a step towards her. 'Is that what the trembling virgin act was all about? Keeping me happy at all costs! You've already demonstrated that you would do almost anything to stay here, even to the extent of taking your clothes off.' He bit off her protest. 'And now you were actually prepared to let me make love to you . . . Love! What a joke!' Horrified, George stumbled backwards, but he caught her wrist. 'Ideals, George, are things people die for.' He stepped towards her, a pulse beating violently at his temple. 'I know.'

George no longer had any desire to explain herself. She was beyond caring what he thought in her need to strike back and hurt him. Cause him as much pain he was inflicting on her.

'Don't be so melodramatic, Lukas. No one in his or her right mind would die to save the world from your calendars.' His grip tightened but she went on recklessly. 'And what on earth makes you think I'm a virgin? I told you I share a house. Bob Turner is one of the men I share with. But there's Jeff, too. And Tatty.' Provoked beyond all reason she added, 'And Alan.'

'Is that all?' he asked, a contemptuous twist to his mouth.

Her violet eyes flashed in the gaslight. 'Jay. Dear Jay. However could I have forgotten him?'

'Easy in such a crush.' The light conversational banter belied the menace in his eyes. George shrank back, suddenly very afraid of what she had done. His fingers bit into her arm as he dragged her close. 'So one more really won't make much difference, will it?'

'Damn you to hell, Lukas!' George struck out blindly and a lucky blow loosened his grip. She wrenched free and ran blindly out into the darkness. She blundered wildly in the direction of the Land Rover, determined to get away. But the dark shape was an illusion and she rebounded from the tearing claws of a thorn bush, hardly feeling the scratches in her panic.

'Oh, God! George! Come back. Where the hell are you?' He was close. Too close. She ran into the darkness, hot tears blinding her to everything but the need to get away from him, the sound of his pursuit only driving her on.

'Georgette! Don't be an idiot. I'm sorry. I didn't mean it. Just stand still, for heaven's sake, and I'll find you.'

She barely heard him, only aware of his voice driving her panic, until a startled nightjar flew up from the path directly in front of her, bringing her to a sudden and terrified halt. The blood was pounding in her ears, her throat tight and aching with the need to scream, and the sure and certain knowledge that she could not.

She stood, rooted to the spot. He had told her not to be afraid. The stars were bright, it was only her fear blinding her. Gradually shapes began to make some sense around her. A thorn bush, with its wicked spikes, darkened against the sky. She could see the fever trees by the side of the river. She heard a small animal snuffling away to her left and her skin crawled, but it moved away, sensing her alien presence.

Slowly sanity began to return and she forced herself to turn around. She had to get back to the camp. If she could make it by herself it would be a victory of a sort. She would drive straight to Nairobi and sanity. As she made a single step in the direction of the camp a bat detached itself from the night and skimmed her cheek. Her scream brought an instant echo from Lukas.

'Stay where you are. I'll come to you.' She could hear him crashing through the bush towards her.

'Lukas!' she screamed again, raw fear blotting out every other emotion.

'I'm coming, George. Don't be frightened, love. I'll find you.' He was closer, she turned to face the direction of his voice. Then he swore and there was another sound. A crash of something heavy falling.

'Lukas?' George strained to hear. 'Lukas?' she ventured again. Nothing.

'Lukas,' she pleaded. 'Please don't frighten me like this.' She attempted a step into the blackness, almost expecting him to jump out at her. Then she heard the heart-stopping sound. A low moan of someone in pain.

She called again, but there was nothing and cold fear gripped her, not for herself this time, but for him. She stood for a moment trying to remember the direction in which he had been coming. She had turned to face him when he called. Slowly, hardly daring to breathe, she edged forward, casting about her to left and right as she went.

'Lukas?' Her voice was little more than a croak. 'Where are you?' She could see more than she had realised, or her vision was clearer now that the panic had retreated in the need to find Lukas and help him.

Even so, she almost missed him. He

had rolled into the darker shade of some overhanging tree, and on to his back. Only the pale reflection from his face attracted a second glance. She crawled over to where he lay and examined him with apprehension. There was already a darkening at his temple from the blow he had received from a nearby rock as he fell. She stood up, casting around her for help, and almost put her foot in the same hole that Lukas must have stumbled into. A closer examination showed that his left ankle was swelling rapidly.

'Oh, my love, what have I done to you?' She bit her bottom lip. There was no one to help her and she'd have to do the best she could and pray it was enough. A splint. She would need a splint. Without hesitation she removed her shirt and, using the long sleeves, tied it in a figure of eight to hold the feet and ankles together. She had nothing left but her bra and she sacrificed that without a second thought, tying his knees together to complete the job.

She leaned over him and checked the pulse at his throat. It wasn't as steady as she would have liked and his breathing didn't sound right. He needed to get to the hospital in Nairobi without delay. His eyelids flickered. He stared up her. 'George? Are you all right?' He made a move towards her and groaned. Relief almost undid her.

'Keep still, Lukas. I think you've broken your ankle. Don't try and move. I have to get back to the camp and find some help.' She was desperately afraid that if she left him she would not be able to find her way back. But she had to try. She stood up and looked round. The small glow from the gas lamp in their tent was clearly visible. She drew an imaginary line from the tent to the tree and set off as rapidly as she dared. If she fell down a hole there would be no one to help either of them.

She pulled a sweatshirt from her bag to cover herself and tried to think what to do next. She had to get him back to camp. With a sudden inspiration she grabbed the bottom legs of a camp bed and dragged it outside. It would do as a makeshift stretcher. If she had the strength to move him.

'*Memsahib*?' Startled, George looked up into the puzzled face of Kubwa. She hadn't time to feel relief. Quickly she explained what had happened and Kubwa carried the bed to where Lukas lay, lapsed once more into unconsciousness. The steward held up the lamp and sucked in his breath.

'Very bad.'

George didn't need him to tell her that. Despite her warning, he had tried to move. Now in the fierce, hissing gas-light Lukas looked like death, his cheeks hollow, yellow under his tan. She checked his ears in the lamplight. At least they were clear, and in any case he would have to be moved. Between them they managed to carry him to the Land Rover.

Kubwa took his shoulders. 'You just look after his legs, *memsahib*. I will lift.'

It was hard. She could see the muscles straining on the man's neck as he lifted the dead weight of Lukas. They propped the unconscious man on the edge of the vehicle between them while Kubwa regained his breath. Then they manoeuvred him inside.

'Thank you, Kubwa,' she said with feeling. Without him she would have had to wait until the others returned from Nairobi, and heaven alone knew when that might be. She packed her patient around with pillows and with a sudden inspiration turned to the steward. 'Can you drive?'

'Yes, *memsahib*.'

'The keys are in the ignition. Take care over the track. We'll put on some speed on the road.'

'I'll take care, *memsahib*. You look after the *mzee*.'

She felt every rut, every bump, every stone as, cradling his head in her lap to protect it from the worst of the battering, they made the torturous ride through the bush. She had soaked a handkerchief in cold water and laid it over his brow.

'Can't you go a bit faster?' George shouted after a while.

The man applied his foot to the accelerator. The jarring to her back increased, but the unconscious man was not aware of it. 'Lukas!' she whispered desperately. 'Come on, my love, wake up. You've been unconscious too long.' She wiped his forehead again, and in a sudden impulse kissed his brow and laid her cheek against his. 'Just wake up and I'll tell you all about old Bob. And the others.' She stroked the hair back from his forehead, wincing at the spreading bruise. 'Can you hear me? I don't sleep with him. He's a sixty-two-year-old hippy, Lukas. You were right, about me, I'm the original panting virgin.' She laid her lips on the still eyelids. 'And if you don't come round I could spend the rest of my life in that state. I need you to rescue me.' She felt the tears running down her cheeks and kissed them away as they splashed on to his face. 'I wouldn't care how many photographs you took of half-naked women. I'd finance the wretched calendar myself if it would make you happy. Just as long as I could come along with you and hold your camera. And share your bed.'

She stared down at him, wondering idiotically if they made double camp beds. 'You're the only man I want. The only man I've ever wanted.' She laid her ear to his chest. It was difficult to tell in the noise of the Land Rover, but his breathing seemed better. 'Lukas?' She stroked his face and after the slightest hesitation kissed his mouth, willing the life back into him.

She wiped the sweat from his face and covered him with a jacket. She hadn't been able to find a blanket. When she looked again his eyes were open. 'Where are we?' he asked.

'Shh, love. Quiet.' But relief rang a peal in her ears and tears of thankfulness ran unchecked down her cheeks.

At the hospital Lukas was whisked efficiently away, leaving George and Kubwa to cool their heels in the waiting room with nothing but a cup of machine coffee to help the time pass.

At last, however, a doctor appeared. 'Your friend will be all right, I think. Concussion, but no fracture, and his ankle is cracked. Did you splint him?' George nodded. 'He's lucky you were there. A drive like that could have caused a real mess.' He suddenly grinned. 'You can have your — er — garments back when you visit the ward tomorrow. Mr Lukas insisted on returning them personally. Rarely have I seen a brassière put to such practical use.' He relented in the face of her anxiety. 'You can have a peek at him before he goes to the side-ward. But be quick.'

Lukas was lying on a trolley, the dressing on his forehead dead white against the sickly yellow of his skin. But he was conscious.

'How do you feel?'

'How do I look?'

'That bad? Better go to sleep.'

'Don't go. Give me another kiss.'

George flamed under the amused eyes of the nurse but pressed her lips against his. It was the least she could do.

'Why don't you stay with him?' the nurse suggested.

'I'll have to tell people what has happened. The rest of the crew don't know where we are.'

The nurse found her some paper and she wrote a brief note for Kubwa to take to Walter, then allowed herself to be led to the room where Lukas had been settled into bed. 'He's asleep already. But if you want anything in the night just ring.' There was an upholstered chair in the corner and, after checking that Lukas was indeed asleep, she prepared to settle down for the night. The girl brought her a pillow and a blanket. 'You'd better have this,' she said, offering her a glass. 'You don't look so good yourself. It's brandy. Purely medicinal.'

'Thank you.' George reached out for it, but found that her fingers were trembling too much to take it. She clutched her arms around her chest and sank back into the chair as she discovered that her legs would not hold her.

'Easy now.' The nurse held the glass and she managed a few sips, the first raw heat choking some life into her. After that she managed to grasp the glass and sipped slowly. Gradually the tremors eased.

'Thank you.'

'All part of the service. I'll bring you a cup of tea before I go off duty. Sleep well.' She turned off the overhead light, leaving only a small nightlight above the bed. George checked him. His head had been patched up and there was a cradle keeping the bedclothes away from his ankle. A long shuddering sigh was wrenched from her as she looked down at the still figure lying there. The white dressing on his forehead was startling against the deeply tanned face. There was a smear of mortar down his neck and she reached out to brush it away, but, suddenly afraid of waking him, she let her hand fall back to her side.

She settled in the chair, but could not sleep. Once he became restless and she was instantly up. He was muttering something and she put her ear to his lips, but whatever he was saying wasn't in English, or any other language that she knew. Gently she stroked his forehead and murmured soothing, loving words to help him rest. Gradually he quietened and she returned to her chair to try to snatch some sleep.

Dark dreams kept her drifting on the edge of sleep, and she was aware of the nurse checking her patient from time to time. Once she woke trembling and sweating. Eventually she drifted off as the sky began to lighten and minutes later, it seemed, the still fresh face of the nurse was leaning over her with a cup of tea. 'Drink this, then you can come along and have a wash.'

'Thanks. I must be filthy.'

Nothing could be done about her clothes. Her jeans were streaked with mortar from her block-laying, and the sweatshirt was covered in dust where she had crawled about in the bush. But the shower restored her and her hair was clean if damp.

'Feeling better?' The nurse nodded without waiting for her answer. 'Make yourself some toast in the kitchen if you want.'

'Thanks, but I'd better get back to Lukas.'

'The doctor's with him.' She smiled. 'He'll be all right, you know.'

'Are you sure?'

'Quite.'

George allowed herself to be led to the kitchenette and the comfort of doing something useful distracted her slightly from her feelings of guilt. She looked up anxiously as the nurse bustled in.

'Can I . . . ?'

'Patience. I'm going to wash him. Unless you'd like to?' she said archly. George shook her head vigorously.

'He's awake?'

'And very cross. Had a bit of a row, did you?' The girl was amused. 'I'll give you a call when he's settled and you can make it up.'

'I've made you some toast.'

'I'll have it later.'

George wandered aimlessly about, wishing there was something useful she could do. But one thought dominated everything else — the fact that Lukas was still angry. Well, she could hardly blame him.

★ ★ ★

'George, my dear. Are you all right?' Walter's concern told her plainly enough that she looked dreadful.

'I'm all right. But Lukas . . .'

'It's that bad? Where is he?'

She shook her head. 'No. No.' She was reassuring. 'They're washing him.'

'He'll hate that.'

George looked at him in astonishment and without warning burst into tears.

'There, there, child.' He produced a handkerchief and mopped her face. 'Better tell me what happened.'

She gave him a censored version of events.

'Lukas clearly won't be fit enough to finish the job. It's a pity, with only one picture left. No MotorPart calendar this year.' Walter sighed. 'It's been a chapter of disasters. I think I'm getting too old for all this.'

'I'll do it. If it will help.'

She saw hope rise than fade in his eyes. 'That's very good of you. But do you think you can?'

'I'm not a complete novice, Walter. I know I laid it on a bit thick to irritate Lukas . . . besides, you've got nothing to lose. If we pack up and go home now, no calendar. If I can complete the last shot at least I won't have messed things up completely.'

'I'll see what Lukas says,' Walter hedged finally. 'Are you coming to see him?'

She shook her head. 'I don't think so. I'll wait here.'

George sat quietly, staring out of the window at the colourful flower-stall, but not seeing anything. Hindsight was very clear, she thought. If she had been frank with Lukas right from the beginning there would have been no room for misunderstandings.

It seemed a long time before Walter returned, and at the question in her eyes he shook his head.

'He won't hear of it. We're to break camp and everyone except me is to leave on the first available flight.'

'But that's silly!' she protested.

'I agree. You might as well have your moment of glory. As you say, what have we to lose? I'll pop in and look at Michael, since I'm here. Coming?' He turned and walked towards the ward. George followed, hiding her anger. He hadn't understood. She didn't want glory. She just wanted to put things right.

'Hello, early birds.' Michael put down his newspaper and greeted them both cheerily, then he gave George a closer look. 'You're looking a bit rough, George. The old man been giving you a hard time?'

George responded with a smile. 'Rather the reverse. He's suffering from concussion and a cracked ankle.'

'He's here?'

Walter nodded. 'They've got him in a room by himself, but they'll be moving him up here soon.'

'Oh, well. It'll be company.'

'Of a sort. He's madder than a wet hen.'

Michael looked at George. 'I won't show him yesterday's paper, then. Have you seen it?' George shook her head. He handed it over with a chuckle. It was a moment before she saw the item that had amused Michael.

Top photographer Lukas, on location somewhere in Kenya with a bevy of beautiful models for this year's MotorPart calendar, has a new assistant. Miss Georgette Bainbridge, daughter of millionaire MotorPart chairman Sir Charles Bainbridge, has moved into bachelor Lukas's two-man tent. Can we assume from this that Georgette — George to her friends — has renounced her long-held radical feminist views? I will keep you informed.

There was a small reprint of the front-page photograph from the week before.

Horrified, George whispered, 'For goodness' sake don't let him see this!'

Michael grinned. 'Keep it as a souvenir if you like.'

'Keep what as a souvenir?' George jumped at the sound of his voice. She looked up to a pair of slate eyes regarding her with extreme disfavour, as his bed was rolled into place alongside Michael. 'So. You've added Michael to your long list of conquests.'

'You'll have to ask him that.' She folded the paper and tucked it into her bag. 'How's your head?'

'Sore.' He reached under his sheet.

'The doc said I was to give you this.' He held out her bra. She made a move to rescue it but he twitched it out of reach and tucked it under his pillow. 'He also said I was to thank you.'

'No, Lukas. Don't do that. It was all my fault.'

'That's what I told the doc. God, I feel sick.'

George moved swiftly, grabbing a bowl from the bedside, and held his head, while he retched painfully. He lay back on the pillow, beads of sweat standing out on his brow and she moistened a tissue from the water-jug and wiped his mouth.

'I'm sorry, Lukas.'

'Are you? Why? You got exactly what you wanted, and now you can go home to Bob.' His mouth turned down with distaste. 'Or was it Alan, or Tatty or Jay?' He lay back listlessly. 'Or all of them?'

'I'll leave you to work that one out. How long do they say you have to stay here?'

Lukas shrugged. 'Does it matter?'

Walter stood up. 'We'd better get off, George. I've arrangements to make.'

'I'll get a paper from somewhere,' Lukas yelled defiantly after them.

Walter's eyebrows rose in enquiry and without a word George handed the paper over to him.

'Are you really a radical feminist?'

'I once demonstrated at a beauty contest. If that makes me one, I suppose the answer is yes. The photograph is from last Wednesday's daily edition. You can't tell from that, but it was a march in support of the homeless.'

'I can see why you might want to keep it from Lukas.'

George smiled. 'Oh, no, he knows about those.' Walter's eyebrows shot up in comic surprise. 'It was the bit about sharing his tent. He wouldn't want it to get about.'

'Perhaps not. Although I should have thought he was immune to this sort of thing by now. He would be more concerned about you, I should think.'

He handed her back the paper. 'I don't know what happened last night, George, and it's probably better if I don't, but Lukas didn't just fall over and crack his head and his ankle. Did he?'

'I thought you didn't want to know, Walter? Shall we get along? We've a lot to do. Did you get the motorbike?'

Walter checked, appeared to reconsider his response and nodded. 'The devil's own job we had getting it over the river, too, on a trailer.' He glanced at his watch. 'I'd better phone your father and tell him what's happened.'

George shook her head. 'No. Don't do that. As far as the world is concerned, if this photograph sees the light of day, Lukas took it.'

'Yes.' He smiled with sudden understanding. 'Boss.'

\* \* \*

The girls were told what had been decided and agreed to keep quiet. Kelly was shown the newspaper gossip piece by the boyfriend and threatened with dire consequences in the shape of bugs in her bed if she passed on any other little items of news. She stared at it in dismay and George felt quite sorry for her. 'I didn't say all that, George. I didn't *know* you were a feminist thingy, so how could I?'

'No, of course not. Just try not to mention me at all. That would be safest.'

'Right. Oh. I forgot. Your horse won!' She produced a wad of notes and handed them over to an amazed George.

'What on earth am I going to do with all this?' She asked. 'I can't take it out of the country.'

'You could hire a proper photographer,' Peach offered.

'Let's get this motorbike shot done,' Walter butted in. 'Then we can all go home.' The others took their cue from him. Except for Peach, who sat astride the gleaming black machine, with a sulk that a three-year-old could have been proud of. George ignored it, concentrating on getting the lighting and angles perfect. Then she fired off a few shots, watching Peach carefully through the lens, knowing that she wouldn't be able to resist the film. Gradually the pout became sultry and exactly what she wanted. She pressed the auto release and the motor-wind did the work.

'That's a wrap,' George shouted and caught a touch of approval in Walter's smile.

'Lukas couldn't have got her to look like that,' he said, helping her with the dreaded tripod.

'No,' George agreed. 'I shouldn't think Peach has ever been photographed by a woman before. I've seen her work with Lukas. She's been told by someone to make love through the lens. It's all right as far as it goes, but it's not real. Now, what she felt today was real.' She grinned. 'I guess I'm just not her type.'

She felt suddenly bleak. Right at this moment, she thought, I don't feel like anybody's type.

# 9

By the time they had finished it was too late to start packing up camp. Walter drove up to Nairobi with the last of the films and to arrange their flights for the following day. He returned late to find George waiting up for him.

'How is he?'

'Looks a lot better than this morning,' Walter reported. 'They had him out of bed in a chair. He still feels sick from time to time, but if you hadn't told me how long he had been unconscious I'd have said they'd have let him out tomorrow.'

George let out a long sigh of relief. 'You told him we were all going home tonight?'

Walter helped himself to a drink. 'No. I said tomorrow. He's capable of working out the logistics for himself. He was as mad as hell that no one had come in to see him.' He looked up and smiled at her. 'No. That's not quite true. He was as mad as hell you hadn't gone in to see him.'

'Don't be silly, Walter.' There was no reason he would want to see her except to tell her what he thought of her. And she already knew that.

'Who's being silly? When I presented your apologies for not coming, because you were too busy, his exact words were . . . unprintable.'

She made a determined effort at a smile. 'That I will believe. I'll get off to bed now. We've an early start in the morning.'

'He had managed to get hold of a newspaper, by the way. He says to tell you that he's planning to issue a further bulletin. George?' She paused and looked back. 'Whatever happened to your spectacles?' He shook his head. 'It doesn't matter.'

She didn't sleep. Instead she lay wondering what she would be doing if Lukas hadn't seen the newspaper. She had meant to retrieve the wretched thing and burn it, but the truth of the matter was that she had forgotten all about it. She glanced across at the empty bed. Would she be lying in his arms over there right now, instead of having a Simone de Beauvoir paperback for company? It was no substitute, she decided.

Furiously she grabbed her book, but she couldn't concentrate on the words. Her throat ached with tears she was refusing to shed and her eyes were continually drawn towards the empty space in her life. She had wanted him so much. Still wanted him. She groaned, hating herself for her weakness.

Morning came as a blessed relief. With the daylight she could leave the stuffy confines of the tent and start packing the equipment prior to breaking camp.

'Where's Kelly?' she asked, as she helped herself from the coffee-pot in the mess tent. She couldn't face more than a piece of fruit, but the others, Kelly apart, were enjoying the usual cooked breakfast.

'She felt a bit sick. I told her to stay put for now,' Suzy said.

'How does she look?' George asked, with a sinking feeling.

'Not too bad, although it's difficult to tell in those tents. Everything looks green.'

'She'll be all right in a bit,' Peach remarked, casually. 'Take her some dry toast. That's about all you can do for morning sickness.'

George's hand shook on the coffee-pot. 'Morning sickness?'

Peach stood up and stretched. 'She'll be doing corsets for the mail order catalogues next year.'

Having dropped her bombshell, she wandered off. 'What a little bitch,' Suzy directed after her, then looked at George. 'Leave her in peace. I'll pack up her things for her.'

'Naughty girl. She wouldn't have come if Lukas had known,' Walter remarked.

'Perhaps that's why she didn't tell him,' George said sharply. 'What would a man know about sacrificing a career to have a baby?' She pulled herself up short as she saw the glint of humour in his eye.

'The newspaper gossips have it right, then. A feminist to the core. I can see why you and Lukas might fight.'

'That's not why we fight, Walter.'

Too late she saw the knowing look. 'No, my dear. I didn't think it was for a minute.'

★   ★   ★

She slept for most of the long haul home. It was getting to be something of a habit, she thought as she struggled to wake in the grey light over London, gathering her belongings together. The others were wide awake and excited. For them the job was finished and they were off to conquer new horizons. George just felt flat.

Henry was waiting at the barrier for

her. 'That's a lovely tan, miss. Had a good time, have you?'

George opened her mouth to tell him exactly what sort of a time she'd had. Then she closed it again. 'Lovely, thank you, Henry.' She looked around. 'Anyone need a lift into London?' she asked.

Kelly had already disappeared in the arms of her beloved John. Peach was being wrapped gently in a fur by a man old enough to be her father. Or possibly even her grandfather, George thought rattily.

'I'm going the other way, but thanks,' Mark said. 'See you.'

George was left with Amber and Suzy, who asked to be dropped at Waterloo. Henry took their luggage and led the way to her father's Rolls.

Once the two women had been dropped at the station Henry turned to George.

'Where now, miss? Paddington?'

'Yes, please, Henry.'

The chauffeur took an envelope from his jacket pocket and handed it to her.

'Sir Charles asked me to give you this. I didn't think you'd want to open it in front of the other ladies.'

George took the envelope. 'That bad?'

'I really couldn't say, Miss George.'

She nodded and ripped the envelope open. There was a note from her father, a chequebook and her credit cards. There was also a newspaper clipping. With trembling fingers she read the note.

Dear George, I suppose it was too much to hope that you could keep out of the newspapers, even at six thousand miles. I assume that you'll have a perfectly reasonable explanation as always, but if you want me to polish up the shotgun just let me know. As you've done everything I asked I am restoring your finances to your own hands. Come and see me as soon as you feel fit to start work. I haven't been idle while you've been away and we've a lot to discuss. Love, Pa.

A tear splashed on to the paper and the ink puddled and ran and then soaked in.

The little house in Paddington was cold and dark. George shivered as she stepped into the hall and over a pile of letters on the mat. As she bent to pick them up she saw the note propped on the hall table. It was from Bob.

'Blimey, miss, it's a bit parky in here.' Henry flicked the light-switch. 'Might be a fuse,' he said doubtfully.

'No. We've been cut off.' She handed him Bob's note and he drew a shocked breath over his teeth. 'It was my fault, Henry. He said he'd stopped gambling, but I should never have given him the money to pay the bill. It was just asking for trouble.' Her letter, urging him to contact Bishop in an emergency, was one of those unopened in her hand. 'He'll be back, full of apologies, as soon as he's won a few pounds.'

'You can't stay here, George.'

The unexpected use of her name by the ultra-correct Henry almost undid her. The temptation to run to Odney, to hide and lick her wounds in the warmth of home, was intense. But she shook her head.

'I'll be all right. I'll sort the bill out and the place will soon warm up.' He was doubtful, but she wouldn't be moved and reluctantly he brought in her bags. 'Tell Pa I'll come to the office in a day or two. As soon as I've caught up with things.'

He nodded and finally left. George toured the house. Apart from dust and dirty dishes and an unbelievable amount of rubbish, it seemed to be in one piece. What it really needed was a spring clean, and for that she needed hot water. She changed into warmer clothes and wrapped up against the biting wind, set off to organise the reconnection of her electricity supply, and lay in stocks of cleaning stuff.

It took two days to work from the top of the house downwards. She was giving the hall mirror a final shine when the phone rang. She lifted the receiver.

'Georgette Bainbridge.'

'George?' Her father's surprised voice asked.

'Hello, Pa.'

'It is you. Are you feeling quite well? I've never heard you address yourself by your proper name before.'

'Oh! Did I? Couldn't have been thinking.' Colour flooded into her cheeks. More likely she had been thinking too much.

'Hmm. When are you coming to see me about this project of yours? I thought you'd be hammering at my door by now,' he teased gently. 'And I'd really quite like to see you. Can you make it this afternoon?'

She caught sight of her reflection in the newly shone mirror and shuddered. Two days of scrubbing and polishing and window cleaning had left the house looking wonderful and George looking a wreck. Her face was yellow and colourless under the tan, and dark rings around her eyes screamed that she wasn't sleeping. She pushed the strands of hair from her face and sighed. 'I think I could do with another day.'

'You are all right? I didn't take any notice of that silly newspaper clipping, George. I only sent it in case you hadn't already seen it. And as for today's little offering . . . '

'There's been another one?' A ridiculous kick of adrenalin set her heart pounding.

'You haven't seen it?' Her father laughed. 'Well, if I seriously thought you'd taken part in some wild native betrothal dance, I should be having a few words with Lukas about his intentions.' He paused. 'I must say, though, that the photograph is quite convincing.' He waited, clearly expecting some response and she forced herself to chuckle.

'Really? I must buy a copy, it sounds highly entertaining. And I should steer clear of Lukas. He was very angry that you dumped me on him, mainly, I think, because the only available space for me was in his tent.'

Her father gave a short laugh. 'He must be losing his grip. The Lukas I know would have been more than happy in such circumstances.'

'Shall we just say that I didn't go out of my way to tempt him?' Her firm control of her voice was beginning to slip and she changed the subject. 'Can we meet tomorrow? Take me out to tea. I've dreamed of it.'

'The Ritz? Four o'clock.'

'Lovely.' She hung up slowly and re-examined her face in the mirror. If her father saw her looking like that he might have second thoughts about what she was doing in the tent of a 'playboy bachelor' in the middle of the bush.

'Well, George,' she said to herself 'you look a mess. Better not let it get to be a habit.'

The phone rang again almost immediately.

'George?'

George smiled as she recognised Kelly's voice. 'Hello, Kelly. How are you?'

'Oh, great. Really great. But I wanted you to know it wasn't me. John won't tell me who gave him that picture, but I didn't know anything about it. Really, I didn't.'

'Kelly, please calm down. I know you couldn't possibly have passed the story on to John. There's only one person who could have done that.' It took a while to reassure her, but finally, after promising to keep in touch, Kelly hung up. George stood looking at the phone, daring it to ring again. Half expecting Lukas to ring to find out if she enjoyed his little joke. Horribly disappointed when he didn't.

She spent part of the afternoon having a sauna and a facial. Then she allowed the stylist to cluck and tut over her hair while a manicurist did what she could with her hands. The following morning she toured the boutiques and treated herself to some new clothes. Real, fresh-from-the-shop clothes. She had forgotten how they felt.

Her father's amazement at the sight

of a perfectly groomed daughter, in a new clinging moss-toned print dress, was repayment enough for the trouble she had taken.

'I have to admit to an anxious moment or two about what you might consider a suitable outfit for afternoon tea,' he confessed. 'I should get cross with you more often. You look wonderful.' Then his eyes narrowed. 'A bit tired perhaps.'

'I've been spring cleaning the house,' she said. 'It was a bit of a mess.'

'It looks as if you've been spring cleaning yourself, too,' he remarked. George started at his perception.

'Yes. I suppose I have. I was a bit of a mess too.'

He waited to see if she would go on, but she had nothing more to say on that score and he gave his attention to afternoon tea. But as she sipped the Earl Grey out of the delicate china she remembered sipping strong sweet tea out of a cracked cup, with Lukas laughing at her, and she knew where she would rather be.

'George? Are you listening?' She dragged herself back to the present.

'Sorry, Pa. I was miles away. What were you saying?'

'Walter brought the transparencies to show me. They're very good. He told me how you helped out when Lukas took that knock.' He smiled. 'He was very impressed.'

'It was the least I could do.' She cleared her throat. 'How is Lukas?'

'Fine, as far as I know. He's away somewhere, I believe. More tea?'

'No.' She shook her head. 'No. Tell me what you've been doing to get my idea off the ground.'

He gave her a considering look and then shrugged. 'I've been talking to one or two people I think might be interested in backing your scheme.'

George allowed him to talk, forcing herself to listen, blanking out the memories that kept trying to intrude. Gradually, her enthusiasm was recaptured and by the time they left the Ritz she had managed to push Lukas into the deep recesses of her memory, something special to be taken out and examined only in the privacy of her heart.

★  ★  ★

Her father arranged for her to have her own office. Sometimes she didn't see him for days, but occasionally he popped his head round the door with a bit of good news, or a fresh idea. Bishop found her a bright young girl from the typing pool who rapidly proved her worth.

A month after her return from Kenya, George Bainbridge could have been mistaken for any earnest young businesswoman in Docklands. Some of her old crowd had reappeared, keen to involve her in new causes. George had welcomed them, but she had thrown herself full time into the project and had little to offer except moral support and a bottomless teapot. Only those who were interested in her refuge project stayed.

'How's it going?' George looked up with pleasure at her father's voice.

'Slowly. But, I hope, surely. That old warehouse is in a terrible mess, but I'm sorting out a scheme to get it put together. We're using out-of-work tradesmen to train some youngsters. If they build their own space it will be something for them to feel proud of.'

'Excellent. I'm glad it's going well for you.' He looked at her with concern. 'Come down to Odney Place this weekend. The girls are bringing the children over. The woods are full of bluebells and red campion,' he added, as if further incentive was required.

'I'd love to. Can you give me a lift down on Friday night?' She looked at the package in his hands. 'What's that?'

He glanced down. 'Oh. It's what I came in for. The proofs to make the final choice for the calendar. I came to show them to you. Perhaps you'll help me decide.' If he saw her hand tremble he made no comment. 'He said there are some photographs you took as well.'

'He?'

'Lukas. He called in this morning with them.' Before she could stop him he had opened the box and started to lay out the proofs across her desk. 'They are very good, don't you think? Which is the one you took by yourself?' She sat unmoving, numb in the knowledge that he had been in the same building and she hadn't known. It was probably as well. If she had known, nothing would have stopped her from flying up the stairs to catch a glimpse of him. Make certain he was well, recovered. 'George?' Her father's voice brought her back to the present with a jerk. 'Which one did you take?' She glanced at the photographs, reluctantly at first, and then with heightened interest as she remembered the ones they had taken together.

'That one.'

Her father looked at her with respect. 'Extraordinary. You've really caught something deep in that girl. When Lukas insisted you must be credited with it on the calendar I thought he might just be covering himself. But this is as good as any of them.'

'No!' Sir Charles looked up, eyes suddenly narrowed, and she realised she had over-reacted. 'I made it quite clear to Walter that I would take it on the strict understanding that no one would ever know.' She retreated in the face of her father's penetrating gaze.

'George, although I'm your father I have left you to sort out whatever has happened between you and Lukas in the way you feel best.'

'Pa . . .'

'Don't tell me that nothing happened. Lukas was as jumpy as a kitten this morning. Almost leapt out of his seat every time the door opened.' He looked grave. 'You're a grown woman and I respect your right to privacy. But I will not have a lovers' quarrel disrupting one of my major public relations campaigns. Sort out the matter of attribution between you without involving MotorPart in anything unseemly. I hope I've made myself clear?'

There didn't seem to be any point in protesting. 'Yes, Pa.'

He nodded and picked up a box of transparencies. 'Can I look?'

'Of course.' She opened one and held it up to the light. Safe pictures of a sunrise. She passed them to her father and he held them up to the light.

'Lovely skies.' He picked up the second box and began to flick through them. 'This must be the school party you were telling me about. Dear God, is this you?' He laughed and handed her the picture to look at. She was surrounded by eager youths, trying to lay a concrete block, just a happy snapshot. She picked up the third and felt weak as she looked at Lukas laughing broadly at something one of the boys had said to him. She pressed her cheek against the heavy glass of the window to cool it. The feeling didn't go away, she discovered. Hard work kept the mind occupied during the day, but it didn't stop the desire burning her up in the night. Her father took the photograph from her limp fingers and examined it against the light.

'I do admire the man. He's done remarkably well for a refugee.' Sir Charles Bainbridge continued to look at the picture, giving his daughter time to regain her composure. 'His parents were killed in a car crash trying to get to the Czech border in '68, when the Prague Spring folded. His grandfather brought him to Britain and raised him. A sad business.'

'I didn't know.'

'I have to pay him the earth to get him to do my calendar.' He continued to look through the transparencies. 'He justifies it because it gives him the time to do other work that doesn't pay well.' He handed her another picture to look at. 'You'd better get him labouring down at the warehouse. If this picture is anything to go by he certainly knows how to work.' Her father turned to go. 'Oh. I almost forgot. He said to tell you that he'll ring you soon about some deal you made. He said you'd understand.' The transparency slipped from her fingers and flickered to the floor. 'George?'

'Yes, Pa. I heard. I understand perfectly.'

'Good. Then I'll see you on Friday.'

The odd thing was that she felt safe at Odney Place. She was sitting with her family around the fire after lunch, knee deep in Sunday newspapers, when the phone rang. There was a general moan of uninterest. She was the nearest so in the end she answered.

'George Bainbridge.'

'Good afternoon, Georgette.' At the husky velvet of his voice she almost dropped the telephone.

'Lukas.'

'You sound surprised. Didn't your father give you my message?'

'Yes. He told me. I expected you to phone me in London.'

'No, not there. I thought you'd probably be busy with Bob. Or Jeff. Or Tatty. Or one of the many others whose names, for the moment, escape me. I assumed that you would be relatively undistracted in your father's house.'

'How did you know I'd be here?' He ignored her question.

'I thought tomorrow would be a convenient day, since you're so close.'

'Close?'

'You're very monosyllabic today, Georgette. It's unlike you to have so little to say for yourself.' She ignored this little gibe.

'How close?'

'My studio is at Cookham.'

'That close?' she whispered.

'Yes.' She heard the laughter in his voice. 'That close. Ask your father to drop you off on his way up to town in the morning. He knows where.'

'Yes.'

'And Georgette, make sure you have an early night. I don't want any dark circles under your eyes.'

'What shall . . . I wear . . . ?' Her voice trailed off as she realised that he had already hung up. She stood looking absently at the receiver. It would hardly matter.

'Who was that?' Her father looked up as she rejoined them in the drawing-room.

'It was Lukas. Can you drop me off at his studio in the morning? He says you know where.'

'No problem.' He paused, but if he noticed the slight flush to her cheeks he said nothing. 'He bought old Dolly Morton's cottage last year. You know where that is, down by the river. He's done wonders with it by all accounts although I haven't been there for a while.'

'Yes. I know where it is. It's a lovely spot.'

Her father waited, then asked, 'Will you be long, or shall I send Henry back for you?'

'No. Don't do that. I don't know how long I'll be. I'll catch the train to town.'

Quite unable to stand so much restrained curiosity, she turned away. 'I think I'll go and see about tea now. Emma? Mary? Who wants to toast muffins by the fire?' Her nieces scrambled up to help and George numbly followed them to the kitchen.

She took herself off to bed early, not because Lukas had given instructions that she should, but because she couldn't bear the normality of the chatter. Her sisters discussing their children's schooling. Their husbands talking about the state of the economy.

And she needed to get away from the watchful eye that her father had kept on her all evening. He knew something was amiss, but he was waiting for her to tell him. He had always waited, and in the past she had gone to him with her problems. But not this time. This time there was nothing he could do to make it better.

# 10

George dressed with the utmost care. It had taken her a long time to decide what to wear. She had risen early and the dogs had greeted her joyously at the unexpected treat of a dawn walk. The trudge through the woods had whipped the colour into her cheeks and despite the lack of sleep she glowed after a fierce shower. Then she had turned her attention to her wardrobe.

Her first choice had been something soft, feminine, to tempt him. To make him want her. She dismissed the idea as unworthy.

Her hand had lingered momentarily on a pair of scruffy jeans and she smiled. Perhaps that was what he would expect. The sight of her face in the mirror, eyes dark with longing, was like a cold douche.

She was going to be photographed by

a man who despised her. Who had extracted a promise that she pose for him in return for keeping a job he had spurned her for taking. Her own feelings would have to be buried deep, hidden completely, or he might extract more from her than she would wish to give to anyone who did not love her.

She made up with a light hand, neither emphasising nor underplaying the features that nature had blessed her with. Perfect for a day at the office, which was where she intended to go immediately he had finished with her. Her hands shook as she put on the severest white blouse she could find and found the buttons oddly elusive. Get a grip on yourself, George, she told herself firmly. It's nothing. Like going to the dentist. That's all.

She examined her rear view in the long mirror. She tugged firmly at the jacket of the navy pinstriped suit bought to impress hard-headed businessmen that she wasn't a dewy-eyed idealist. Not that she would need to impress Lukas with that fact. He was already convinced. Nevertheless she was satisfied with the overall effect. She picked up her document case and joined her father in the dining room.

He raised an eyebrow at her outfit. 'You look as if you're about to take on the entire board of the Bank of England.'

She poured herself a cup of coffee, looked him in the eye and smiled. 'Good.' It hadn't taken a genius to work out how Lukas had known where she was. Only her father could have told him.

Half an hour later, George walked by herself up the path to the cottage door, her suit a poor substitute for courage. She took a deep breath and put up her hand to the knocker but the door opened before she touched it.

'Georgette. You came.' The bruise had gone from his temple. Only a small scar remained to remind her of the worst night of her life.

'Hello, Lukas. How are you?'

'Quite recovered, thank you.' He looked her up and down, a slight smile curving his lips. 'You'd better come in.' She hesitated for just a moment before stepping into the hall. 'Would you like some coffee?'

She shook her head firmly. 'No, thanks. I have to get on.'

The hesitant smile disappeared. 'In that case you'd better get out of that armour plating you're wearing. Stewart will do your hair and make-up.' He opened the door to a small dressing-room, but she made no move to enter. They had made a deal. No one was to be here but the two of them, and he had broken it. Lukas saw her hesitation. 'He'll go as soon as he's finished. We could have managed the make-up, but I'm hopeless with hair,' he apologised.

'I seem to remember you were pretty handy with hairpins,' George retorted coldly, but there was no point in making a fuss. Just like the dentist, she reminded herself. Grin and bear it.

'Miss Bainbridge? Come on through.

I'm Stewart.' He took her jacket and swathed her in a huge pink cotton garment. 'Make yourself comfortable. It won't take long.' He examined her make-up. 'Very nice. I'll just give it a bit more intensity — the lights tend to wash you out.' He flicked colour on with a series of brushes and, apparently satisfied, turned his attention to her hair.

He brushed out the neat chignon over which she had taken so much trouble and spread her hair over her shoulders. Then he took small portions from each side to plait and loop behind with narrow green velvet ribbons. When he had done that several times he smiled. 'Your dress is in the cupboard there. I'll leave you to it. Bye.' Stewart left and she heard the outside door of the cottage bang and a car start.

George did not move. A dress? What sort of a dress would he have chosen? She looked at herself in the mirror. 'Any dress, George, is better than none,' she reminded herself. And she had been expecting none. But then perhaps he would expect her to take it off. Reveal herself bit by bit. 'Stop it!' she snapped at her reflection and shook herself firmly. She opened the door, then stood regarding the garment that hung there with nothing short of amazement. It was white muslin, its full sleeves caught tight above the elbows and at the wrists with the same green velvet as she wore in her hair. The neck was scooped, but hardly revealing, and the waist high, gathered below the bust with more green velvet and tiny silk flowers. She took it from its hanger and found that she wanted, more than anything, to put it on.

She removed her clothes and stepped into it. She managed the top hook, but gave up the struggle after that, instead turning to examine this new image of herself. The reflection that gazed back from the mirror was so different from the young woman who had left Odney Place that morning that she could hardly be recognised.

'Are you ready?' He tapped at the door.

'Yes. No. Just some problems with the hooks.' He opened the door and then halted, his face like stone. 'What's wrong?'

He shook his head and walked slowly around her. 'Nothing. Nothing at all. I can hardly believe how well it has worked.'

'It wasn't what I expected,' she prompted him.

'No. Because you never allowed me to finish what I was saying.' His smile sent her heart-rate up several notches. 'But you came anyway. Turn around and I'll do the hooks.'

'I came because we had a deal.'

'So we did. And you're back in your father's good books, I see.' The hooks were awkward and he stood pressed against her back for agonising moments, as he struggled to fasten them. She remembered the smell of his cologne, but the musty, sweaty smell of Africa had been washed away. Today he was back to the well-groomed Lukas, devastating in a black open-necked shirt and trousers, hair trimmed and firmly under control. She wasn't sure she knew this Lukas at all. 'There, all done.' He took her hand and led her through to his studio.

'I want you to stand there, so your face is lit by the natural light from the window.' He frowned. 'Hold on.' He disappeared and returned moments later with two three-foot-high lilies. 'I didn't forget, you see. Madonna lilies. I knew they would be perfect. Hold them . . . yes, like that. I'll take some Polaroids.'

She gazed absently out of the window at a clump of bluebells growing under a hedge in the garden, trying to work out exactly what was happening.

'Come and look, George. See what you think.' There was nowhere to leave the lilies so she held them gingerly to the side and leaned over the table to look at the Polaroids. 'Well?' She looked up into his eyes. Teasing eyes, and today the blue was dominant.

'You want the truth?'

He looked surprised. 'Of course.'

'I think I look an absolute idiot.' For a moment shock replaced the humour in the depths of his eyes. They stared at one another with complete and absolute antipathy. Then, without warning, he laughed.

'Oh, George, Georgette, my love. You are quite incorrigible. I turn you into a Byrne-Jones fairy queen and all you can say is that you look an idiot.'

George turned away, well aware that a deep flush was suffusing her neck and face. 'Perhaps I just feel more at home in a pair of jeans. This isn't me.'

'You looked very at home in that suit. Absolutely terrifying.'

'That's just work. And if you've finished having fun with me I do have a busy day ahead.'

'No. I haven't finished. You promised to sit for me, and sit you will. And there are certain other items of unfinished business on our agenda.'

'Unfinished business?' She trembled and she silently cursed the flowers for betraying her.

'Back to your place.' He turned her around and gently patted her bottom. 'There's a good girl.' He sighed. 'Do you think you could hold those flowers a little more sensitively? You look as if you're about to crown me with them.' He bent to look through his view-finder.

'Don't tempt me, Lukas.'

'They would at least do less damage than the last time.' He straightened. 'Why did you run away?'

She looked at her feet, at her hands, anywhere but at him. 'I didn't run away. There just didn't seem to be any point in staying. I salvaged what I could out of the mess and left before I could do any more damage.'

'Your father tells me you refuse to be credited with your picture.'

'You've spoken to him again?' She shrugged. 'You know my feelings. It was bad enough working on the wretched thing. I won't have my name attached to it.'

'And I absolutely insist that you do. It was not my photograph, George. I refuse to have my name on it. You have no one but yourself to blame, you know. I told Walter you were not to take it. I knew how you felt. I should have known you would have to play the martyr.' He went on hurriedly as she began to wave the lilies threateningly. 'Besides, I've thought of a way around it.'

'Of course there's a way around it. Say you took it.'

He shook his head. 'And help you off a hook of your own choosing? Never. Besides, I believe you're making a great deal too much fuss considering your offer to personally finance the next one.' The touch of triumph in his voice brought her up short.

'I beg your pardon?'

But he had returned to the contemplation of his camera. 'Look a bit to the left, will you? Chin up.' She heard the motor wind stop and turned back angrily, but he was smiling. 'Your exact words — correct me if I'm wrong — were, 'I wouldn't care how many photographs you took of half-naked women. I'd finance the wretched calendar myself if it would make you happy'.' He raised a questioning brow. 'About right?'

Her breathing was too quick. 'You were conscious?'

'Semi-conscious, I suppose. Drifting. Coming round. I could hear. You told me about your hippy pensioner. You promised to tell me all about the others. But you didn't come back,' he added reproachfully.

'You told me to go home to . . . all of them. So I did.'

He was dismissive. 'It took a day or so for my memory to reassert itself. Bits kept floating back. At first I thought I had just dreamt it all. But I remembered the kiss. I remembered that very clearly. Just keep looking like that.' He pressed the remote switch and again the motor-wind drove the film on. 'Just keep looking like that.' He walked swiftly across to her and lifted her chin with his hand. 'Always look at me like that.'

His mouth caressed her lips so gently that she scarcely felt their touch, but when he stepped back she moaned, leaning towards him, letting the lilies fall to the floor.

He caught her shoulders and held her at bay. 'You'll understand my surprise at hearing you confess to being the 'original panting virgin'. Especially since you had gone to such great lengths to convince me that you were not.'

She coloured. 'You were going to do something about that.'

'It's on the agenda, my love.'

'At the meetings I go to everyone has a copy of the agenda, so that we know where we are.'

'I'm making it up as I go along. Put it under 'Any Other Business'. Does that sound right?'

'Perfect. But you mustn't let people linger over unimportant items.'

'Because you have a busy day ahead of you?'

She put her arms around his neck and pulled him down to her. 'Oh, yes. Without doubt. The busiest.'

With a fierce groan he swept her up into his arms and carried her up the narrow stairs, pausing only to kick open the bedroom door and set her down. Then he began, without haste, to unhook the fastenings that held her dress together.

It was too slow. Georgette shivered, every part of her responding as his fingers brushed against her skin, igniting the desire that she had kept damped down for far too long. There was no hesitation now. Only the impatience for discovery. Her dress fell in a heap at her feet and she stepped free of it, adding her remaining garments to the pile. She turned for his inspection. His eyes were all the words she needed and she held out her arms to him, offering herself without reservation.

'You're beautiful, Georgette. Clever. Kind. And beautiful. It's too much in one woman.' He buried his head in her neck and began to trail kisses down to her breast.

'You've forgotten 'rich',' she groaned.

'I don't give a damn about your money. Give it all away.'

'Oh, Lukas. That's what I've been trying to do.' She laughed. 'That's just what I've been trying to do. But can we talk about it later?' She began to undo the buttons of his shirt. With a harsh, grating breath he dragged her to him and carried her across to the bed.

'You witch. I'm being taken advantage of. All you want is my body.' He tore off his clothes and lay down beside her.

'I'll let you know,' George murmured and pressed against him, feeling the rough hair of his chest against her breasts and the hardness she wanted so much. She ran one hand down his spine, drawing him close and gasping with raw pleasure as his tongue laid siege to her mouth and his hands began a gentle exploration of her body. A soft moan escaped her as he took a proud rose-coloured nipple between his lips and grazed it with his teeth, then continued downwards, trailing kisses across her taut body. He returned his attention to her neglected breast and drew it hungrily into his mouth. She whimpered, arching towards him, the ache between her thighs desperate for a release that only he could give her.

'Lukas, please . . . ' she begged him and he groaned, easing himself between her legs, until he was where she wanted him. For a moment he held her against him, close and still. She didn't hear the soft cry deep in her throat as she moved desperately against him. But he did, and, responding to the desire that had darkened her eyes, he gradually began to move within her, stoking the fire, setting her alight, until they matched one another in a wild surge of passion, Lukas driving her to dizzy heights of pleasure that she had not dreamed possible. Then, when she thought nothing more was possible, he lost control and they fell together out of their depth and floated downwards into a bottomless sea.

When they surfaced the phone was ringing. Lukas leaned across George. 'I'm sorry. If I don't answer it will go on forever.'

She buried her face in his warm shoulder, finding pleasure in the touch of his skin against her own. He raised himself upon one elbow, kissing her very deliberately and, without taking his eyes off her, he lifted the receiver. 'Lukas.'

He smiled as he listened, experimenting with butterfly kisses to her eyes. 'Sorry, Charles. Georgette won't be able to make lunch.' George gasped and made a grab for the phone and he rolled on top of her, pinning her arms beneath him. 'Besides, we've already eaten.' He glanced at his watch. 'Yes, I suppose it is a bit early. But we were hungry, and if you'll excuse us, we're just about to start dessert.' He dropped the phone back on the cradle and then he had second thoughts and removed it. He released George, who had been beating against his chest without any success. 'Will he be shocked, do you think?'

'He's been polishing his shotgun for weeks,' she replied, breathlessly. 'Now what did you say about dessert?'

'You're shameless. It's quite shocking how pleased you look with yourself.' He rolled on to his back and pulled her on top of him, delicately licking her nipples. 'Whatever happened to that tiresome and slightly batty female who drove me mad in Kenya?'

'She's still about somewhere. Just below the surface. Looking for a new hat, I shouldn't wonder. I rely on you to keep her at bay.'

'Quite a job,' he laughed softly.

'Full time,' she promised and allowed her hands a little exploration of their own.

He drew in a sharp breath and caught her hands and held them captive in his own.

'Didn't you like that?' George asked, innocently.

'Later, my sweet. While I recover my strength you have a little explaining to do.'

She looked thoughtful, and then smiled. 'What do you want to know?'

'I know all about Bob. But who the devil are Tatty, Jeff, Alan, and Jay?' He rolled over on to his side. Still holding her close.

'Where shall I begin?' She grinned down at him.

'Jeff?'

'Jeff is an out-of-work miner from the north-east. He came down to London looking for work, but he needed an address, somewhere to put his head down. The girl at the Job Centre sent him to me.' She grinned. 'He has a wife and three children. He's gone now. He found a job and his family have joined him.'

'I'm glad to hear it. And Tatty? That's a very odd name.'

She giggled. 'He's covered in tattoos.'

'Covered, George?'

She lowered her lashes. 'So I've been told.'

'Hmm. What about Alan and Jay?'

George looked momentarily serious. 'I still have to do something about Alan. He's a fourteen-year-old living rough on the Embankment. Sometimes I can persuade him to come home for a meal and a wash and with luck he falls asleep on the sofa. I've tried to get him to go home, but he won't.'

Lukas shifted and began to toy with her breast. 'I'll have to see if I can help. And Jay?'

'Yes, Jay.' She rolled over on to her back and stared at the ceiling. 'Jay is my biggest problem. He can't be left, you see. He needs a permanent home and I've promised I'll always keep him with me.'

Lukas turned her face towards him. 'He'll have to live with us, then? When we're married? Not exactly what I'd had in mind.' He dropped a kiss on to her lips. 'I hope he won't be too intrusive.'

George heard the words, but could hardly bring herself to believe them. 'Married?'

He propped himself up on an elbow and looked serious. 'Yes. It's an old-fashioned custom, but still currently in use, in which two people swear to love one another until the end of their days. It also has the magic effect of changing the female's surname to that of the male involved, thus solving the little problem of the attribution of the calendar. If we're both called Lukas, no one will know who took what picture.'

'That's not a very good reason to get married, Lukas.' She frowned. 'Haven't you got another name? You can't be just Lukas.'

'Not one that anyone, except my grandfather, has ever called me, and he's dead.'

'I'm sorry. Pa told me about . . . what

happened to you and your family. I understand what you meant about ideals . . . '

He quietened her with a long and lingering kiss. 'It's Karel. Not ideal for a nine-year-old boy going to a tough London primary school. Better forgotten.'

'But that's so sad,' Georgette murmured. 'Karel.' She tried the name.

Lukas groaned. 'I don't care what you call me. Just say you'll marry me.'

She sighed. 'But Jay . . . Are you sure you want to give him a home? He can be an absolute nuisance at times.'

'Georgette, I've known you a very short time, but long enough to know that if you make a promise you keep it.'

She stared at him in amazement. 'You really mean it, don't you? You'd take in some waif from the streets, sight unseen?'

'If you're part of the bargain. I discovered very quickly, my love, that while life with you may have its ups and downs I cannot imagine living it without you.'

'Did it take you a whole month to

decide that?' she whispered.

'Oh, no. After I had kissed you, that was never in doubt. But I had commitments. Michael and I went off to Sudan to take some photographs for Save the Children. What a pair. Two good legs between us.'

'Lukas!'

'It set the ankle back a bit, and frankly the thought of making love to you without all my faculties was enough to make the strongest man tremble.'

'Silly. I'd have helped,' she teased.

'Then I was so mad with you that I sent that photograph to the *Chronicle*. Were you angry?'

'Only that you didn't telephone to gloat.'

'May I take that as an acceptance of my proposal? Or shall I go down on one knee?'

She gave him a lingering kiss. 'I'm tempted.' He groaned and she laughed. 'Perhaps not. I'll take the bent knee as read. It seems a little out of place after what we've just done.'

'Nonsense! Have you no romance in your soul?' He leapt out of bed and, taking her hand, went on one knee.

'Miss Georgette Bainbridge, will you do me the immense honour of marrying me?'

She lay back, helpless with laughter. 'Get back in bed, you'll catch cold,' she gasped.

'Put me out of my misery first,' he demanded.

'Yes, yes, yes! Oh, Lukas. I love you so much.' She buried her face in his shoulder as he returned to the warmth of her body. After a while she raised her head and smiled. 'And I know Jay will be so pleased. He doesn't take up a lot of room, Lukas. In fact he's been living in the office since I went to Kenya, but the cleaners hate it. And his language has always been a problem. Heaven knows where he picked it up.'

'He lives in the office?' Lukas looked temporarily lost for words.

'But you've been to the office. You must have seen him.' She gurgled, barely able to contain herself. 'In Bishop's office. My parrot . . . ' She squealed as he grabbed her. And then she didn't say anything very much for quite some time.

* * *

'Ladies and gentlemen. It is a very great pleasure to be here this afternoon to officially open the refuge to which my daughter has given so much of her time during the last few months.'

'When she first told me about her plans I was so much against them that I made the somewhat rash move of sending her to Africa to get over it. As a result of that I now have a son-in-law and a grandchild very much on the way.' Sir Charles Bainbridge looked at the couple beside him and smiled. 'Not that I'm complaining.' The residents of the converted warehouse officially called the Docklands Re-settlement Centre, but known to everyone simply as 'George's', gave a rousing cheer.

'You've all worked hard and with great enthusiasm to bring the centre to fruition. I hope it will provide shelter and temporary housing for a great many people, and give those of you who started it a launching platform for a better future.' He beamed around. 'Now isn't it about time we broached the beer?'

The party was in full swing and nobody noticed when George and Lukas left.

'Satisfied, Georgette?'

'Mmm.' She was thoughtful. 'I was just wondering. Now we've got Alan settled with Jeff and his family, we really ought to be doing something for the rest of those children.' She placed her hand on the bulge below her own breast. 'What do you think?'

Lukas stopped and turned. 'This is it, isn't it?' he asked. 'For the rest of our lives?'

She laughed softly. 'Do you mind?'

'No, my love. We have so very much, after all.' And he kissed his wife quite thoroughly to prove it.

We do hope that you have enjoyed reading this large print book.

Did you know that all of our titles are available for purchase?

We publish a wide range of high quality large print books including:
**Romances, Mysteries, Classics**
**General Fiction**
**Non Fiction and Westerns**

Special interest titles available in large print are:
**The Little Oxford Dictionary**
**Music Book, Song Book**
**Hymn Book, Service Book**

Also available from us courtesy of Oxford University Press:
**Young Readers' Dictionary**
**(large print edition)**
**Young Readers' Thesaurus**
**(large print edition)**

For further information or a free brochure, please contact us at:
**Ulverscroft Large Print Books Ltd.,**
**The Green, Bradgate Road, Anstey,**
**Leicester, LE7 7FU, England.**
**Tel:** (00 44) **0116 236 4325**
**Fax:** (00 44) **0116 234 0205**

## DANGEROUS FLIRTATION

### Liz Fielding

Rosalind thought she had her life all mapped out — a job she loved, a thoughtful, reliable fiancé . . . what more could she want? How was she to know that a handsome stranger with laughing blue eyes and a roguish grin would burst into her life, kiss her to distraction and turn her world upside down? But there was more to Jack Drayton than met the eye. He offered romance, excitement, and passion — and challenged Rosalind to accept. Dared she?

# ROMANTIC LEGACY

## Joyce Johnson

Wedding plans in ruins, Briony Gordon immerses herself in her job as senior wine buyer at Lapwings Wine Merchants until a dramatic turn of events forces her to reconsider her future. A substantial legacy from her beloved Grandfather gives her the incentive to explore new possibilities. At Moonwarra winery in Western Australia, Briony finds feuding brothers quarrelling over the Winery's future — a future which gives her a wonderful business opportunity and where she finds true love . . .

# CONFLICT OF THE HEART

## Dorothy Taylor

A summer job, as live-in nanny, caring for seven-year-old Ellie seems like a dream for Karen Carmichael. But while Ellie proves a delight, her father, archaeologist Neil Oldson is hard to get to know. Karen puts his reserve down to pressure from the looming deadline on the nearby Roman site he is managing. But when valuable finds from the site are stolen, her growing feelings for him are thrown into doubt. Then Karen's life is put in danger.

# TOPAZ ISLAND

## Patricia Robins

Phillida Bethel's first holiday job is mother's help to beautiful Suzanne Kingley on the exotic Topaz Island. But she could never have guessed that danger, romance, adventure and excitement are to come her way — in full measure. And her inexperience leaves her with no yardstick by which to assess the fascinating American boy, Jeff Aymon. It is the English student, Greg Somerville, who seems the only safe haven in a world of beauty which suddenly turns sinister . . .

# UNDER THE AFRICAN SUN

## Ginny Swart

Whilst on her Gap year, Patsy Whittaker travels to Cape Town to visit her elderly great-aunt Grace. After a break-in at the shop Grace runs, Patsy convinces her mother Maureen to finally return to South Africa to help out. Whilst there, both mother and daughter find reasons to stay on longer than intended — but Daniel Clayton needs to convince Maureen she really is the one for him, and Patsy suspects that her new man isn't all he seems to be . . .

# A FRAGILE SANCTUARY

## Roberta Grieve

When Jess Fenton refuses to have her disabled sister locked away, her employer turns them out of their cottage. Wandering the country lanes in search of work, they find unlikely sanctuary at a privately run home for the mentally ill — the very place that Jess had vowed her sister would never enter. As she settles into her new job, Jess finds herself falling in love with the owner of Chalfont Hall, even as she questions his motivation in running such a place.